Broken

Billie Dureya Shell

BROKEN

This Book Is Dedicated

To the memory of my cousin Shatwan Ward
I love you and will miss you...
You'll never be forgotten.

ACKNOWLEDGEMENT

Once again I want 2 give thank 2 God for this gift I am so grateful for him giving me away 2 provide 4 my family in my house we will alwayz put you first.

To my mother Mclessie Shell you taught me so much and you loved me NO MATTER WHAT I love you so much momma.... What's up on with some bake chicken LOL☺.

To my little sister Glenda I love you and miss you blackie get at ur big brother Lil Sis.

To my Wife Shatoya Shell you get on my damn nerves but I wouldnt trade you 4 anything. In the world I love you more then words can ever express.

To all my children I love y'all Jazmine, Ant'Tuan, Davon, Anthony, David, Lil Dureyea, Alura, Queen Diavion, Cameron, Preniece, Shaniece and Tajh I love u all and I'll 4ever have ur back you all give me a reason 2 smile.......... to my cousin Zane RIP nigga I miss u more then anyone will ever no, your always remembered love you bro.

To my cousin. Ty I miss you thank 4 looking out 4 me and Zane you played a big part in my life and I always looked up to you l love you... Uncle Woody I miss you and love you, you no your my favorite uncle....

To my nigga Jamal love you, my brothers Lawrence and fred thank 4 showing me the game I love yall 4 that.

To my old est sister Nedra love you thank you 4 always having my back. to my family uncles anties cousins etc.. I love y'all even those of you that act funny as fuck

To my dark side niggas y'all no what it is YAAH GANG........

Now to all my readers and fans I love you thanks for reading I hope u enjoy this book as much as I enjoy writing them with this Corona Virus 19 shit there ain't shit to do but write so I'm on my shit with that being said y'all be safe cover your face and love each other life is short so love the ones that really love you I'm gone enjoy the book

AND STAY SAFE

Author

Billie Dureyea Shell

THERE'S NOTHING U CANNOT DO IF U PUT UR MIND 2 IT ....

All you nigga got EDD money so aint no excuse why you can't get a book LOL

Team Shell

PROLOGUE

RING! RING! RING! This damn phone just keep ringing and I am tired of answering questions. Malcolm, Deena, and I have been in this hotel room going on two weeks and I was feeling like a damn criminal. Fuck! Who was this calling I picked up my Iphone 4 and looked at the caller id, I really needed to download an app that could block calls. It was an unknown number that made me skeptical to answer. My grumbling stomach made me forget about the phone. I hadn't eaten in two days. Thank God the kids didn't have school, but I couldn't help but think what was I going to do? It had been two weeks since Hakeem had died. Two long weeks of out of control arguing, fighting and I did not think that my kids could take any more of it. For heaven's sake they had just lost their father and all people could do was argue. Fuck them where was everyone at when I really needed them. I had to get this call and start answering and stop ignoring people they were not going to keep punking me. I slid the phone to answer. "Hello," I barked with plenty of attitude. Hell, I was tired of the drama whoever was calling me was about to get cursed out something I should have been doing. "Oh yes Ms. Turner?" It was a male's voice he sounded kind of shaky I guess because of the way I answered the phone. I calmed my tone down. "Yes, this is her." Lord I hope this is not the police. I didn't do anything wrong it was an accident. "Ma'am I am calling from Global Life Insurance. It seems that your significant other Hakeem Moore has passed away?" "Yes sir," what I thought to myself? Insurance Hakeem stupid ass had an insurance policy? "Well, Hakeem Moore had named you as sole beneficiary so we would need for you to come in the office and fill out some papers so that we can discuss your payout." Insurance money! Oh yes Lord! Who knew Hakeem actually had some damn sense. And he named me sole beneficiary. Yes! He should have after all the years of his bullshit! My kids were still sleep but they had to wake they asses up we were getting paid. "Give me the address." I said quickly as I grabbed the pen off the nightstand with the paper. I had been writing down shelters that the kids and I could go to. He gave me the address and I hung up the phone. I ran to the bathroom and went to pee. Oh yes Hakeem better had a good insurance policy. Hakeem damn I missed him I mean we had our problems, but he was the only man I had ever loved, and he was the only man I knew he was my kid's father and now I was a single mother. Well technically I had been a single mother since the kids was born except for the fact that Hakeem was a great provider but other than that he never really dealt with the kids. He adored our daughter Deena and would sometimes spend quality time with her but Malcolm our son the time spent was something that I had to pressure him to do. It was never just because it always had to be a reason. But he was gone now, and I had to put my big girl panties on. Hakeem had saved me from a fucked-up situation, but he only did that so he could destroy my world. I didn't want things to end the way they did but it was either me or him, glad I am still standing!

I was on my way to work and I was once again late. I had two write ups already at work and I really didn't know what I was going to tell my boss. I was half-way thinking fuck that Walmart while also realizing I should have stayed in school. My dream was to own my own plus size boutique and I was going to school and working my ass off until last year that is when everything at home started to fall apart. I was 22 years old and I still stayed at home with my mother. I stayed in a kids size bedroom that I really needed to upgrade. As I got dressed, I looked at my size 12 frame in my floor length mirror. My once size 8 frame had widened, and I knew that it was because of the stress in my home life. My mama Lisa stayed getting on my nerves. As I looked at my gorgeous face, I wondered did men see the internal pain that I suffered and ran away. I thought I was cute enough. I was 5'8 I had a nice shape although my hips and thighs had started spreading my waist was still slim. I had a short haircut which I felt fit my pretty light skinned face. Yup I was a redbone. I didn't have a bad reputation of being a hoe and I was proud of that. I was having sex, but it was not by choice. I was in a messed-up situation at home, I wonder if guys could see my scars although they were on the inside. I hurried out the front door I had to get gas, so I went to the gas station on 27th street. I was surprised no one was at the gas station it usually be having plenty folks out here. I pulled my two door Pontiac Sunfire to pump number 3 and turned off the car. It was the middle of May and it felt good today. I looked in the mirror and checked my face, my individual lashes were getting old I needed to get them done and I touched up my red lipstick. As I stepped out the car, I was happy no one was out here because the stares made me uncomfortable. I got enough unwanted attention at home. I told the cashier ten dollars on pump 3 and turned to walk out the gas station. As I was walking out the gas station there were three guys walking in. One of the guys was light skinned with big sexy lips, he was fine, those damn gray eyes were hypnotizing so I looked and then looked away. He looked at me also, but I could not hold the stare. I didn't want him to think that I was approachable. The other two guys were light skinned also but big lips was the sexy one, one of the guys had dreads and when I walked pass he grabbed my arm. "Hey lil mama." He said I snatched my arm away and hurried out the door. Being aggressive like that frightened me. Shit you would be a bit afraid if you was going through half the shit that I was going through. I started pumping my gas and I saw that they were heading back out and they were parked at the pump next to me. Hopefully he would leave me be. I acted like I didn't see them and just kept pumping my gas. I looked up and there was sexy lips standing next to me. He didn't scare me he was too fine to scare me. "What's your name?" He asked. His lips were moist too and his gray eyes were hypnotizing. "Niya." I muttered I barely was able to speak. He looked me over and smiled. That smile melted my heart. "Niya, my name Hakeem, can I get your number?" His sexy voice asked but it was more of a demand to me. "I can't really give out my number." I whined and I thought that would end the conversation. He got to looking down at my hand. "I don't see no wedding ring," he said. I still didn't say anything, "look we can just be friends if you want but I see it in you that you need someone like me in your life." I was hesitant but I gave him my number anyways. He was cute and he was right I did need someone in my life. I felt so alone that sometimes I wanted to kill myself, but I knew if I did that then I would be giving the devil what he wanted. I know I had a bigger purpose in life. I went to work and sat at the cash register and daydreamed about Hakeem he was just too sexy. I was happy as hell that no one said anything about me being late. I think my manager was kind of sweet on me and I was happy that he was there and not that trick Sheila. The customers were of course getting on my nerves it was like they were taking their anger out on me. I needed to really get my shit together. I was twenty- two no kids I need to be in somebody's university getting my education. But no, I needed money I needed money to get out of my mother's house. It was a must. I usually would get drunk when I got off of work so I wouldn't have to deal with the bullshit I just hope James wasn't there when I got off. I didn't get off until ten that night and I was tired. And since it was so late at night, I hadn't made it to the liquor store. I called my best friend Mya while I drove home, She answered on the first ring. "What are you doing?" I asked her. Mya and I had been friends since we were in Middle

School. "Shit arguing with Chris stupid ass!" She yelled in the phone. Uh-oh they always arguing but she loved him so what could I do. "Oh, ok girl just call me back or text me" I said getting off the phone. I did not want to hear that shit on the phone. I made it home fifteen minutes later and my heart sank. Here we go again James was here and my mother was not. James was my "mother's boyfriend" and I use that term very loosely. And I say that to say this he is supposed to be my mother's boyfriend, but he is fucking me. Yes, that is right my mother's boyfriend is having sex with me. The sex that I had with James was not consensual. I had nowhere to go and with the little checks that Walmart gave me, I wouldn't be going anywhere, anytime soon. I tried to go to hotels and motels every now and then but right now that was not an option because I did not have any money. I walked in the dark house and I closed the door quietly. I heard my phone go off. Damn! I looked at my phone it was a text from Fred this guy I had been talking to for about two months. Last week he had invited me over and since I was bored, I decided to go over there I needed a break from my home life. Fred was fine 6' 3 a big light skinned ass nigga that was full of life. He had worked at Wal-Mart with me, but he got fired on some attendance bullshit, but he wasn't tripping because he had a little hustle. He lived in a little ass studio apartment which was better than nothing. I sat on his bed. He had a little music playing in the background a little bit of R. Kelly and you know what that meant. No lie he was fine and if situations were different then I would have jumped on that dick, but it is what it is. He handed me a mixed drink. I didn't know what was in it and I didn't bother to ask. I gulped that shit down to relax me a bit. He sat next to me and went straight for my lips. He was kissing and me and I felt uncomfortable. You would have thought that the drink was good enough to get me in the mood but wrong. I know he felt how tense I was, and he didn't even stop. When he tried to unbutton my pants, I flipped out. I started screaming and telling him to move. Fred jumped up like I had lost my mind. I didn't mean any harm, but I just wanted him to get off me. "What the fuck wrong with you girl?" He asked. "Nothing look I gotta go." I hauled ass so quickly out of there that you would have that I was a damn track star. He kept texting me asking me was I okay, but I would ignore it all the time. Hell, no I was not okay. I was twenty-two years old and I was getting sexually abused by my mother's boyfriend. Of course, Fred didn't know that. Fred hadn't done anything wrong it was me I was a mental wreck, all because of James. James wasn't that much older than me he was 33 years old and he wasn't a bad looking guy. But my mother wasn't a bad looking woman to be fifty. She was fit and in shape I definitely got my looks from her. She was a redbone also and she always kept herself up. So that is how she could get younger men, but the problem was younger men seemed to be attracted to younger women, this younger woman. Hakeem These niggas were taking all fucking day and I was not in the mood. I told they ass to be on time. Talking about they want to go in business with me the fuck I look like and these niggas called me to come take they broke asses to the gas station. While I waited on them to come outside, I decided to call Sylvia. She was a little bitch I was fucking on. The hoe was a butherface yeah everything about her was cute but her face. I got tired of that dumb ass Cedes she was never going to come to her senses, so I was like fuck it. I had been waiting on that dumb bitch to realize wasn't nothing like dick, but she wanted to bang pussies. I really wanted to be with her and my kids but the minute she left me I knew the bitch was not loyal. Who the fuck would leave me? She had to be crazy standing 5'11, light skin with gray dreamy eyes. I was the man and on top of that I had curly good hair. Muthafuckas always asked me if I was mixed hell nah straight nigga. Josh ugly ass finally made his way to the car with Elijah in tow. "Damn niggas what the fuck were y'all doing I gotta check on my workers at my cleaning company and y'all taking all day." "Hakeem shut up and just take me so I can get some gas for my car." He demanded. I started laughing as I drove to the gas station. How the fuck you run out of gas and your car parked that's some dumb shit. As soon as I saw shorty at the gas station, I had to have her. That nigga Josh called himself grabbing on her and the look in her eyes was not like she was rejecting him but like she was scared. When she locked eyes with me, she had a look of lust. She was fine with the perfect complexion. I loved dark skinned bitches but that A'Niya was a fine redbone. Her ass and hips was out of this world. Nowadays niggas be wanting skinny bitches, but I liked any size shit as long as she had a pussy to dive into then I was good. When she gave me her phone number, I was happy like a kid in a candy store. I wanted her bad. It was just something about those hazel brown eyes that had me going. As soon as I got in the car Josh hating ass had to say some th ing "so you got her number?" he asked. I ignored his bitch ass and sped off to his house. Now these niggas knew good and damn well I did not fuck with th em. I had l iv ed in the hood true enough, but I had ne ver touched a ny dope or anything like that. I wasn't no soft ass nigga, but I wasn't no damn drug dealer neither. My sister Quita had made sure once I got out of college that I was set to start my business. My cleaning service Moore's Clean was the start of my empire. I had five workers right now and we cleaned residential and commercial properties. You know how trifling muthafuckas would leave they shit after they got evicted and I was there to clean that shit up. I wasn't rich off the shit, but I was making some dough. I was doing better than these nickel and dime ass niggas that was for sure. I dropped them niggas off back at Josh's house and kept right on going. I was already late for a job. Although I had workers, I loved to get my hands dirty too. I loved the idea of being a working man. My father was like that he was a working man and I know that I made him proud. Well I hoped that I did. I pulled up to the commercial property that we were supposed to clean. I saw Rick, Neil, Tim, Steve, and Zach doing the damn thang and clearing shit out. It was time to get to work and make sure them niggas were getting the shit done right.

Chapter Two

ANIYA

My mama brought James home one night a year ago after she had gone to a bar. He was fine he had long dreads and he was brown skinned. She walked in the living room and I was still up eating fruits watching television, I had just got off work hours earlier. I had my robe on and my hair tied down with my scarf. When they came into the living room, I felt naked she should have told me she was bringing someone home she didn't know how I was dressed. He gave me the once over and I must admit he was fine. I could see the lust in his eyes as he licked his lips. No lie that shit set my little kitty on fire, but I was not going to act on it ugh he was my Mother's boyfriend. They went to her room and I guess they had sex. Well I know they were having sex because I could hear all her screams and moan. I rolled my eyes and focused back on the television. I was a bit jealous because my ass wasn't getting none but whatever if I wanted some, I could call any thirsty nigga in my phone and get it. It was a couple of months after she had brought him home that he came on to me. I had saw the lust in James's eyes for the longest and I knew that he wanted me but never in a million years would I think that he would try anything. My Mom worked overnight and one night she left for work and James must have knew she was gone I heard knocking at the door around eleven o'clock. I didn't know who it was I was getting ready for bed and had just gotten out the shower I walked to the living room and yelled "who is it?" "James. Niya is your Mom here?" James was pretty cool at that point. Although I had seen the lust in his eyes he had never done anything inappropriate. "Hold on." I said as I went to put on some shorts and a beater. I went back and opened the door. The cold hit my nipples and made my little titties hard. I opened the door and his dreads were hanging down from his head he looked drunk I could tell he was. "Naw she not here James she had to work tonight," I said opening the door. He walked in and closed the door. He was kind of stumbling behind me. "You okay James?" I asked. He was drunk as hell I could smell the liquor through his pores. "Yeah shawty I'm good," he said sitting on the couch. "I came to get my charger your mother said it was in her room." I walked to the back to get his charger from my Mother's room. I walked back and James was sleep sitting up on the couch. The only light on in the house was coming from the television. I walked up and stood in front of him. "James here you go." I said tapping his shoulder. He looked up at me. "I bet that pussy taste good," he said looking at me. My assumption was that he was so drunk he thought I was my mother we did look a lot alike. He had never made any advances at me, so I didn't think anything about it. I mean he had looked at me with lust, but I could have been mistaking the look for lust and it could have been something else. "James it's me Niya." I said thinking he was confused. "I know." He said grabbing my pussy. It felt good but I was not going to tell him that. "James it's time for you to go!" I yelled. He stood up and he wasn't taller than me he was my height. All of a sudden, he grabbed me around my neck and started choking me. I started trying to fight him, but it was no use he was strong. His strong grip was making it very hard for me to breath and I just knew at any moment I was going to die. I didn't understand why James was doing this to me. "Calm down Niya." He choked me all the way up to my bedroom. Every step was a bit of relief but as soon as we got to the top of the steps his grip got back strong. Oh no not again I thought as we went headed to my bed. James was going to rape me! I was panicking but there was nothing I could do. "Please don't rape me James." I mustered through his tight grip. My heart was pounding. I was all sweaty and it was making me want to fight. But how he had held my neck I knew that that was not an option. When we made it to my bedroom, he threw me down on my bed. "Calm down ma." He said and sat next to me. I tried to get up. "Lay your ass back down." He said and he got on top of me. His sweaty stinky body was making me feel sick. Ugh I did not care how fine he was shit I did not want to have sex with him, and he had sex with my Mom. Noooo! I was thinking but I knew damn well not to say it. "Please don't do this James." I said again as tears started streaming down my face. I thought maybe the tears would make him feel sympathy, but he didn't give a fuck about that. He started kissing on my neck and it felt good, but it was wrong. My body started to loosen up as my juices started to flow and I kept thinking this was so wrong. I couldn't do anything about the way my body was responding. "Calm down," he said while kissing my neck. His voice was low and sexy, and I really started dripping. Damn what was he doing to me? His hands moved down to my pussy. He put his hands in my shorts and felt my naked pussy since I didn't have any panties on. "Ummm you was waiting for me." He moaned. He started fingering me and I could tell he was loving my wetness. "James don't do that." I said through my moans oh it felt good. I grabbed his hand for him to stop. He got up off me and sat up. I let out a sigh of relief and thought good, I thought he was done. But I was wrong he turned and slapped me so hard I know I had a bruise. My light ass skin I knew I had a damn handprint, ugh I wanted to fight his ass but I knew he would beat my ass, so I just grabbed my face and sat there. "Shut the fuck up and I ain't gone tell you again." James pushed me back on the bed and spread my legs. Surprisingly he didn't penetrate me he just ate my pussy and I must admit it was good. I was moaning so loud I could not help it. I mean the way his tongue met the center of my hole and went in and out. Then he licked my clitoris and sucked it so hard that my damn orgasms were sending all types of convulsions through my body. If a muthafucka was looking in they wouldn't even think I was getting raped it just look like I was getting some good ass head and I was. Yes, although I didn't want it James had given it to me, and I liked it. Every time after that he slowly got me ready for sex with him, he was molding me, and I was losing my mind. It felt like rape it did because I knew it was wrong, but it really was good James was really good in bed and although we would fight every time before sex, and he would beat me and threaten me once he put it in it felt great. I know my Mom knew James was raping me, but she never said anything just like when I was seven years old. She would just roll her damn eyes at me whenever she saw him leaving my room. We never had the perfect relationship, but the bitch could have said something to her nasty ass boyfriend. I was pissed that she didn't say anything but most importantly I was hurt. I walked in the house and James wasn't in the living room. Good I thought maybe he had drunk himself to sleep. Lately he had been drinking a lot. I guess the pressures of hustling was getting to him. James thought he was hot shit because he was a damn flunky for some nigga who was the kingpin of the streets. Ha, that nigga was a lame and couldn't even get hoes that was the reason he was raping me. I walked up the stairs to my room. And when I got there, there was James on my bed. I rolled my eyes and I felt so much hate building up in my body that I did not know what to do. Yeah James was fine, but he looked like the devil to me right now. I was not in the mood to fight I was tired. I had just worked an eight-hour shift and my damn feet hurt. After dealing with those rude customers at Wal-Mart I did not want to deal with James, but I had no choice. So instead of even getting mad I just unbuttoned my pants and walked over to him. "Hey sexy," he said as I got to him. I didn't say anything I just laid on the bed. "You must have missed daddy?" He said as he put his dick in me. Oh, it felt so good I thought as I closed my eyes. Although it was rape, I cannot lie James dick was big and he knew how to work it. As he pumped in and out, I was crying yet moaning at the same time. I grinded myself underneath him to make him cum faster I just wanted it to be over. "Yeah you love this dick, don't you?" He asked kissing me. This nigga really thought that I was his girl or something. After he finished, I went downstairs and got in the shower I was crying. I wanted this to be over I didn't know why this was happening to me. It felt so good, but it was so wrong that is what made it so hard because the sex was good, but I knew it was bad. This had been going on for a year now and it was tearing me up. I had dropped out of school and I couldn't date because every time I tried; I would be afraid to meet the guy I was living in hell. Not only because of this but also because this wasn't the first time my mother's boyfriend had raped me. Here I was 22 years old and helpless. James told me no one would believe me because I was an adult. Hell, he was right if they didn't care about a seven-year old girl being raped then why would they believe an of age adult. I was tired I just wanted to sleep I scrubbed my body so hard that my entire body was red. I cried as soon as the water hit my body and I knew that I was living in hell. After about 30 minutes of being in the shower and getting myself together I went in my room. When I got to my room James was still there. Huh what the fuck was wrong with him he usually left and went to my mother's room. I went and sat on my bed and stared at him. "I bought you something, he smiled. That was another thing he stayed buying me stuff jewelry, shoes, clothes, he even gave me money dirty bastard. He was a drug dealer, so I know he had money, but I was starting to think he was doing the drugs he was selling. I mean he was wrong for having sex with me but over the last couple of months the nigga had become delusional because he was acting like I was his girlfriend. Yeah, he was doing more than just selling that dope he was definitely smoking it. He pulled out a box with a ring in it. That ring was expensive too. His sick ass was trying to propose to me! "What the fuck is this James?" I asked rolling my eyes with much attitude. I thought he was going to slap me, but he didn't. "I think we should make this official you should be my wife." He said smiling. This muthafucka had to be crazy. You see what I mean he had to be doing powder, dope, coke or whatever the fuck he sold. "James you are raping me, we are not in a relationship you are dating my Mom ugh." I said rolling my eyes. James brought me back to reality when he slapped me. Yup he was in charge. "See bitch I tried to be nice put this muthafucking ring on," he screamed grabbing my hand he damn near broke it. "I love you Niya and I am tired of this shit in the morning we telling your mother that we getting married and that's the end of this shit you hear me, hoe?" I could not believe this muthafucker was in love and thought we were in a relationship. I was crying and scared. What was I going to do? He was serious too this muthafucka is obsessed with me. He act like this shit was okay and it wasn't. "Stop crying lay down and go to sleep." I laid down out of fear that he was going to hit me. He put his arms around me as if we were really a couple James was a sick son of a bitch. I did not know what I was going to do. My mama was going to be mad. She really liked James and she knew nothing about him raping me. Well she pretended not to know most of the time. She was so happy when he was around that I didn't want to rain on her sunshine. I cried myself to sleep that night cuddled up with my Mother's boyfriend. The next morning when my Mother got home James went and told her that he and I were getting married. I heard a bunch of yelling. I didn't know what they were saying but I knew one thing my Mom was pissed. I don't think she was mad that he was raping me more so that he wanted to marry me and not her. All of sudden the arguing stopped, and I thought I was going to hear James coming out of her room; but I heard soft moans ugh they were having sex. Ugh he thought it was okay to have sex with both me and my Mom and she was allowing it. I could not believe this shit was happening to me. I put on some clothes and decided to go over Mya's house this was just too much. They were having sex so he wouldn't hear me leave. Although Mya and I were friends she didn't know the crazy life I lived. How could I tell her what I was going through I just pretended everything was fine. James had given me forty dollars before he had went in the room with my mother to get my nails done so Mya and I went to get our nails done. I know Mya knew something was wrong with my home life she would always say Niya what's wrong you can talk to me we have been best friends since Middle School. But life had definitely gotten too crazy for me. Thank heavens for make-up to hide my bruises. I always had fun with Mya she made me forget my troubles at home. It was like I was a regular young lady who was free to do whatever I wanted. Truth was I was being held captive by my mother's boyfriend. The girl talk was definitely a breath of fresh air and it made me feel normal. I had been gone for two hours before James decided to call me. "Hello." I answered he had been doing this for the last couple of months calling to see when I would be home. Most of the time I wouldn't answer, I should have known things were changing because he really did check on me like I was his woman. "Where the fuck you at Niya? It don't take that long to get your nails done." I did not respond, "bitch do you hear me!" "Yes, I'm with Mya." I rolled my eyes Mya's green eyes were staring at me. Mya was so beautiful I see why she had a real man to love her. She was light skinned like me, but she had green eyes. Her mother was white, and her father was black. She had beautiful curly hair that was so long and shiny it looked like a wig. Yup she was perfect. "Bitch bring your ass home!" He yelled into the phone. He got on my nerves. "Mya I am about to drop you off I am about to go home." I said wrapping up my food. We had stopped at McDonalds and got something to eat. "Is that your new boyfriend?" She asked. I didn't tell Mya about James whenever she would ask, I would make it clear that he was not my boyfriend. "He is not my boyfriend!" I yelled I was irritated, and I didn't mean anything by it. "Well you always jumping up to go whenever he calls; he is somebody special." "You don't know what you are talking about so just shut up and let's go." I really didn't mean to get mad at Mya I guess I should have just told her what was going on but I was too embarrassed. We pulled up in front of her house. "I am sorry Mya I just have a lot going on." "Well I suppose to be your best friend so why you can't tell me exactly what is going on? I tell you my business because I feel like we are friends and I know you would never tell anybody, but you never tell me what is really going on with you. Do you not trust me?" I saw tears in her eyes which caused me to cry too. I loved Mya but I just didn't want anything to change between us. I did not want her to judge me. "One day we will have a talk Mya just not right now okay honey." "Okay well I am here whenever you need me." The words she spoke was 100% genuine and I had no idea at the time.

Chapter Three

ANIYA

I walked in the house and my Mom and James were eating at the kitchen table. She looked up at me and her eyes were glossy. I felt her pain, but she didn't feel mine. She rolled her eyes with an attitude and looked away. "Where the fuck you been?" James questioned me. I walked in and sat at the table the sick bitch wanted us to eat at the table like we were family. My Mom looked pretty she had on a blonde lace front. She looked like she had been crying though. "What's wrong Mom? Did he hit you?" I asked I worried about my Mom and how she was feeling about this whole situation. I know she loved me. And I was sure that she didn't think I really wanted James or maybe she did we never were close. She just made sure

I had a roof over my head, she didn't protect me. As far back as I could remember she never helped me get dressed for school, she would comb my hair to make sure I was presentable. She never expressed that she loved me. She never hugged me nor showed me affection. "Now you know I would never hit your mother baby." James said kissing my hand. This sick muthafucker did not understand he was ruining my life. I snatched my hand away. "Bitch you done lost your mind! Tell her Lisa tell her to respect her man." The audacity of him to tell my mother to obey him he was sick, but the sick part was what she said out of her mouth. "Respect him Niya he loves you!" She yelled through tears. He never hit my Mom, so I didn't know what hold he had on her. She did whatever he said without hesitation. I looked at their crazy asses and rolled my eyes. I had to get away. I was gaining weight from this bullshit I was going through. Every day it was getting worse and worse. I would eat to drown out the pain I was feeling I knew it was not healthy. After I ate, I went upstairs to my room and saw that I had a text. I didn't recognize the number. I texted back "who is this?" before I knew it had fallen asleep. The next morning, I had to be up at 8 in the morning because I had to be at work by ten thirty. James had gotten in the bed with me and I do not know when that was. I didn't even feel him get in the bed. Luckily, he didn't touch me or anything he just was laying in my queen-sized bed with me. I went to take a shower and put on my uniform. "Where the fuck you going?" James scared me as I came back into the room. I breathed deeply and rolled my eyes. "To work James," I said damn he was nosey like he really was my man. "Oh, okay boo give me a kiss goodbye. I will see you later I will cook for you okay." He said smacking my ass. Ugh this dirty muthafucka. It pissed me off that he thought we were together. I gave him a kiss and left for work. I did not want him to slap me around for work, so I just did what I was told. I was so tired at work I could barely concentrate. I had rested the night before, but my mind was tired. I wanted my life to be different, things had to get better. It was a short day for me at work so that was good. It was almost time for me to go when I recognized a familiar face. It was the guy from the gas station. He was in my line and when I got to him, he smiled. "Hey beautiful," he said handing me the condoms he was buying. I turned my nose up, he was a player. That turned me off ugh but there was still something that I really did like about him. He had something that I wanted. "Hey," I said. "I see you didn't text me back." He stated. I thought about the text I received last night that must have been him. I hadn't even charged up my phone. "Your husband wouldn't allow it, huh." I looked down at the ring at disgust. "No, it is nothing like that I am single I just wear this ring sometimes." I took the ring off. I don't even know why I still had it on. I guess because if James was to see me with it off, he would have beaten my ass so I just left it on so I wouldn't forget. "Oh, okay I ain't tripping cause I want to pursue you." His comment made me smile. "What time you get off?" I looked at my watch, "in 15 minutes, why what's up?" I asked. "I wanted to go catch a movie you down?" He questioned I looked up at him and he made me feel safe for some reason. I didn't even know this guy and with all the shit I was going through I didn't know if I could trust him. "Don't trip I will give you all my information you don't have to be afraid," I must have looked afraid. "Okay but I will have to go change first." I said looking down at my work clothes. "That's cool just make sure you call me okay." "Okay I will." I said and I had planned on it too. The plan was to go home get dressed and leave right back out. It would be good to go on a regular date and be a regular woman. I knew James was at the house, but I was going to go out. Lately James had been over every day and my mother was no where to be found. When I walked into the house, I wasn't surprised to see him sitting on the couch watching television. I walked right past him to get ready for my date. As I walked up the stairs James followed right behind me. I didn't care I was going to leave. I started picking out my clothes and James stood by the doorway. "Where you going?" "With Mya," I lied as I continued to pull out clothes. I could feel his eyes all over me. I was determined to leave. As I looked through my underwear, I could feel James walk up on me. I continued to do what I was doing. He wrapped his arms around me and kissed my neck. "You not going nowhere," he whispered in my ear. I was angry when he said those words. I was leaving I pushed James away from me. "Yes I am!" I yelled walking away. James was quick as he pulled my hair and threw me to the bed. I screamed but he didn't care. He choked me as he pulled off my clothes. I started kicking my legs and he squeezed harder. "Bitch I will kill you today," he growled in my ear. The tears started streaming from my eyes as James inserted his dick inside of me. He wasn't gentle with me today he was rough. As he fucked me it felt like my soul left my body. I couldn't keep dealing with this. He was hurting my body, my soul, and my mind I had to get away. After he raped me, he cuddled behind me. I cried myself to sleep. I was awakened by a call at one in the morning. I looked around and James was gone. I did not know where he was, but I was happy that he was gone. I looked down at the ringing phone, and it was an unsaved number. "Hello." I whispered. "Ay shawty what happened to you I had been waiting for you to call me." It was Hakeem. "I'm sorry I fell asleep." I said and that was true. "Well how about you come and fall asleep next to me." He said. And although I was skeptical, I really needed to get out the house. I agreed and grabbed me some clothes real quick and headed out the door. I did not want James to stop me this time. I needed to get away. I mean really get away. On my way to Hakeem's house my mind was all over the place. I didn't know what I was going to do. I had been getting raped for the last year and I was tired of it, I mean really tired of it. Here my stupid self was on the road to a man's house that I didn't know. But it felt right I needed to get away and right now I felt like this was my escape. I made it to Hakeem's house and my mind was racing. He opened the door and my mouth fell open in shock. Hakeem I had sent shorty a text and she had responded asking 'who is this' but that was it. I didn't know what was up with her and after waiting an hour for a response I decided to hit Sylvia up. This bitch was so annoying asking me to take her ugly ass out. I had backed off of her for a while, but now I needed something to fuck.

'Wyd' I texted. 'Nothing waiting for you to text me.' She responded. I smiled because that bitch was so desperate. I was fine as hell though, so I knew bitches wanted me. One thing about me was I was a one-woman man and I needed a special lady Sylvia was just here to satisfy my needs for now. 'Oh really,' I responded back. 'Yeah I am gone get right to the point Travis I am pregnant.' I had to re-read the damn message again. I know damn well this bitch was not pregnant. Hell nah I was not having that shit. I had told her my name was Travis so there was no way that she was going to get give birth to my child. I just wanted to fuck the bitch from time to time, she wasn't up to my standards. 'Abortion,' was my response. I was sitting on my couch nervous as hell I did not need no more kids I didn't even take care of my three by Cedes but I had good reason shit that hoe, had played me left me so she could do it by herself her and that dyke bitch she was with. 'Yup five hundred should be good' I knew damn well that the damn abortion shouldn't be that much but fuck it I would do anything to get rid of her. 'K drop it off tomorrow.' I texted back. I was done talking to Sylvia and my mind drifted back to the sexy A'Niya. I was a bit mad because shawty had stood me up, but I had to call her and check on her it was just something about her. When she answered and was whispering talking about, she wanted to come over I knew something was wrong. As soon as I saw A'Niya I was like damn she could have cleaned herself up. Her damn hair was wild for it to be short shit she could have done something quick to that shit. "Damn shawty I knew you had just woke up, but I would have waited for you to fix yourself up." I laughed I thought it was a good joke but shawty got to crying and shit. "Calm down it was a joke, I was kidding" I grabbed her and let her in "come on in." After about twenty minutes and three beers later she had calmed down. Even though she was looking fucked up she was so damn pretty to me. Man, when she opened her mouth to tell me the fucked-up shit, she was experiencing I could not do anything but get mad. She told me her mother's boyfriend was raping her and thought she was his bitch. Man, that was some sick shit another muthafucka would be skeptical thinking she was lying but I could tell by the look in her eyes that she was telling the truth. I had red in my eyes and she looked scared. I just couldn't understand how the fuck a nigga could rape a female and force her to be with him and then her Mama wasn't even doing shit to help her. I looked at her and knew I had to make her mine. "That's a dirty muthafucka shawty and your mom not doing nothing about it?" I questioned her.

She shook her head no. I was feeling pissed and I could still smell the sex on her. That shit was pissing me off, "shawty you go ahead and take a nice hot bath I gotta make a run." She looked at me like I was crazy, but I quickly went into my room and grabbed my car keys. I didn't say anything as I walked out the door. She was still sitting on the couch looking confused. When I got in my car, I had to calm myself down. I looked in the glove compartment for my asthma pump. I hated this punk ass asthma, but I had to live with it. I know I was worked up and my chest had started tightening. I didn't like for people to know I had asthma because it was a weakness to me. I knew where shorty lived because after our encounter at Wal-Mart, I had followed her when she got off work. I wasn't a stalker or no shit like that I just wanted to make sure she lived in a good neighborhood. I usually didn't even tell bitches where I stayed or my real name, I was just crazy like that. Not since Cedes I couldn't put my heart in that position again, but I think that Niya would be the perfect lady for me, loyal. As I drove to her house, I knew that this would make her forever mine. I didn't want to tell her what I was going to do because she might try to talk me out of it. I parked in front of the house and jogged to the front door. I was pumped up and ready to whoop some ass. I hadn't whooped no ass in a long time, so I was ready. I knocked on the door hard as fuck a muthafucka was sure to think I was the police. There was no answer, but I know they were in the house because there were two cars in the driveway. Oh, they wanted to play. I tried the door and to my surprise it was unlocked Niya must have left it unlocked when she came to my house. I went into the nicely decorated home and made my way up the hall. I could hear some talking. I bust through the door and I saw a lady who had to be Niya's mother sniffing some powder up her nose. Oh, that would explain it the bitch was getting high. That is why she couldn't handle the situation, but I could. The nigga James stood up and was looking like he wanted to do something. He was a scrawny ass crackhead looking ass nigga. I didn't know why she was letting this nigga rape her. A'Niya's mother was a pretty lady that let me know that she would age gracefully. "Who the fuck is you?" James yelled out. "A'Niya is my bitch," I told him. The anger in his eyes was apparent and he tried to run towards me. I was too quick for the nigga though. I ran straight to him and knocked him off his feet. He must have been high too. Niya's mother was screaming and shit but I couldn't understand what she was saying. I started punching that nigga all in his face and I drew blood right away. I was beating his ass real good and he wasn't even trying to fight back. I didn't know what type of shit this was because most muthafuckas would fight back but he didn't even seem like he felt the blows but the blood covering his face was a tell, tell sign that I was fucking him up. After about five minutes I got up off him and kicked him in his face. Niya's mother was sitting in the corner saying a prayer. Yeah, the crazy bitch needed to say something because she was one sorry piece of shit.

Chapter Four

HAKEEM

When I got back from whooping that piece of shit James ass I walked into a quiet house. I didn't know where A'Niya had gone but I made my way to the bathroom. As I pulled the door open, I smiled she was in the tub asleep, she was beautiful. My presence woke her up. "I am sorry I must have fallen asleep." She said trying to cover her body, but I had seen every curve and I loved it. "Don't worry you can come lay down when you get ready." I had blood on my clothes, and I was ready to get in the shower, but I wasn't going to rush her. She got out of the tub and I went to take me a shower. After my shower I got in the bed next to Aniya. She was soft and smelled good. I snuggled up close to her and she was crying. "Don't worry baby girl I got you." I know she was thinking about all the shit she was going to have to go through, but I was willing to get her through it. The next couple of days we got to know each other. Things were happening fast for us and I loved waking up to a beautiful woman like Aniya. I told her about my dreams and my goals. She was excited just like me and I knew that she was going to be my rock and the person to grow and build my empire with. She was sexy and although we hadn't had sex, yet I knew that once we did it would be just what a nigga needed. After washing Aniya's clothes for the last couple of days she told me she wanted to go get her clothes from her mother's house. I told her I could have just bought her everything new but she insisted on getting her stuff from there. Shit that was cool with me that would save a nigga couple hundred dollars. We made our plan to go get her stuff that evening. Aniya still had a key, so we walked right in the house. The way her body shuddered with fear made me angry. If we saw that nigga James, I was going to beat his ass again just for making her so scared. The house was quiet as we passed the living room. Then we heard some noise coming from the kitchen. Aniya looked at me and we tiptoed our way to the kitchen. I wanted to make sure we knew who was all in the house too. I didn't want that nigga James to sneak up on me. As we peeked into the kitchen, we saw her Mother snorting powder. The look of shock that came over Aniya's face let me know that she did not know her mother was on drugs. She quickly turned and ran up the stairs. All the movement caused James who was sitting at the table to look up. He jumped up when he saw me. "What the fuck!" He yelled. I raised my shirt up so that he could see the .45 that was under my shirt. I didn't even have to say anything to him he knew what was up. "Aniya baby hurry up!" I hollered throughout the house. I kept my eyes on James as I waited for Aniya. Her mother hadn't moved from the spot at the table. She was so high that I don't even think she noticed I was there. It didn't take Aniya long to come down the stairs with her stuff. I would have held her bags, but I had to keep my eyes on the pussy nigga James. I wasn't turning my back on him, I backed out of the door the entire time watching him. As soon as we got in the car, I looked at Aniya and she looked scared as hell and nothing had happened. "You okay baby?" I asked her. "Yes," she nodded her head. I could tell she was trying to understand what she had just seen. "I'm gone take you to the house. I want a nice meal when I get off work tonight." I told her as we sped away from the house. Aniya nodded her head.

"Whatever you want baby. What you want to eat?" "Some spaghetti, garlic bread, and a salad." "Umm that does sound good," she smiled. I was happy that I took her mind off of what she had just seen. When we pulled up to the house, I gave her a couple hundred dollars to get the food. I had to get to work. I kissed her cheek and watched her walk in the house. I had to smile as I drove off. Aniya was a wifey type of woman, she listened well. She had been through a lot, so I wanted to give her a chance to heal. I had stopped fucking with Sylvia after I gave her that money for the "abortion" she claimed she was going to get. My sister Quita told me that hoe, was known for telling niggas she was pregnant to get money out of them. Oh well that was a loss of five hundred dollars. But I just could not take the chance that she was pregnant. I already had three boys that I did not want. I pulled up to the downtown offices and hoped that this day went by fast. I went up to the fifth floor the doctor had hired us to clean their offices and I loved it. It was all types of nurses and doctor bitches that looked good as fuck that I was trying to fuck on. Shit I wasn't even pressuring Niya about no sex because I didn't want it right now, I wanted her to understand that I was here for her and that it was not about sex. I was going to have her ass wrapped around my fingers.

ANIYA

Hakeem was a real gentleman and I was happy to have him or so I thought but now seven years later I had to stop and wonder. I had to wonder why was my life so hard, I cried, I screamed, I prayed, and yet I still went through so much pain. To be honest my five-year-old son Malcolm was the real man in my life. At five years old he had endured a lot. And it was my fault for not leaving Hakeem and allowing my children to see so many things, but I am not perfect, no one is. Hakeem definitely was not perfect oh yes, he seemed perfect but the things that seem too good to be true usually are and the people who seem to be perfect are like makeup. Yes, makeup makes you look good when you put it on but there is no telling what ugly scars you are hiding underneath. Hakeem had two sisters Chiquita and Vanessa. I had met them about a month or so after we started dating and they loved their baby brother. Their mother had died so they made sure they took good care of their baby brother Hakeem. Vanessa was a 5' 10 brown skinned stud, she had a low haircut just like Hakeem. She looked good as a man. She had a girlfriend Cedes and she was gorgeous. She was beautiful like a model. She had long jet-black weave, her brown skin was flawless she didn't need any makeup. For her to have three kids you could not tell because her body was flawless not a stretch mark on it. Chiquita was the eldest of the three siblings. She didn't have any children Hakeem said she couldn't have any kids. Chiquita was brown skinned also, and she was a big woman. Chiquita was a very loving woman I thought when I first met her and over the years we grew somewhat of a bond. But now that Hakeem was gone, I guess she felt no reason to pretend to like me. I remember the day I met them. One Sunday afternoon Hakeem walked in and said get dressed. "Where we going" I asked. I had been getting prepared for work since I had to be there in an hour. "To my sister's house" Hakeem went over there every Sunday, but he had never invited me. Hell, we were in a relationship and we had never had sex. He treated me like his woman, but he didn't make advances at me and I appreciated that, but I was starting to wonder about him. I guess he was trying to let me get over the James ordeal and frankly I was over it. "I have to be at work in an hour. You usually go by yourself." I said following him into the bedroom. We shared a typical male bedroom he had neutral colors on the spread, a dresser, and big television. I didn't have many clothes, so my stuff went in the dresser while he put all of his clothes in the closet. "Well call in I'm ready for you to meet my family." And just like that I picked up the phone made an excuse and called in. I liked Chiquita and Vanessa we hit it off right away. But Cedes was the bitch I did not like. She kept looking at me the entire time it wasn't like a jealous look I don't know what kind of look it was, but she was pissing me off. Later I would find out that it was a look of sympathy, yes, she knew all too well what I would endure. When we got home, we sat and watched reruns of Martin and cuddled. "Did you used to date Cedes?" I asked Hakeem. I don't know what made me think that, but the question popped up in my head. Hakeem looked at me with surprise. At dinner I had noticed he tried not to look at her, but she was so beautiful you couldn't help but stare. That's how I knew she was staring at me because I was staring at her. "What! Did that bitch tell you that shit!" He jumped up and screamed. He was angry and I did not understand why. "No! No calm down." He sat back down, "I was just asking because she seemed uncomfortable around you" which was true she didn't even look his way the entire time we were having dinner. "Oh, shit she just weird like that." He said and that was all the explanation I got and at the time I was okay with it. I felt like Hakeem was genuine so whatever he said I was agreeing with it. The man had just saved me there was no reason for him to lie to me. Plus, we had never mad our relationship official. He had told me a lot about himself already. It was just him and his two sisters they mother had died a couple of years ago. He had never really said what happened and he never mentioned his father. I assumed he just didn't know his father. That was the situation I was in I didn't know my father and my mother never explained why I didn't know him she just kept it simple, he gone she would say.

Chapter Five

HAKEEM

When Niya had asked me about if I used to date Cedes, I damn near jumped out my damn skin. We were all cuddled and watching t.v. and my dick was on brick. I had fucked a bitch Juanita from the doctor's office earlier that day but shit Niya was still looking and smelling good. I know I needed to make her wait a bit longer, but this shit was getting hard. I definitely had to turn up my game on bitches so that I could fuck them and forget all about fucking her. When I took her to meet my sisters, I wanted to get a feel of her around my sisters. Of course, Quita was acting like she was the best fucking big sister ever that ol crazy bitch. Cedes was looking at me all sad and shit like she wanted to say something to me, but I didn't want to hear shit. I had been told her to make sure she did not tell her damn kids that I was their daddy. Fuck that I had told Niya I didn't have any kids and that is how I wanted to keep it. Cedes knew what would happen so she knew better than to say anything. So, when Niya had asked me that shit I just knew that bitch Cedes had somehow told her. Yeah that bitch must have forgotten about those ass whooping I used to give her. Even though Niya said that Cedes didn't tell her that I made it my business the next day to pay that bitch a visit. Yeah, she thought I didn't know their schedule, but I knew every fucking thing. Nessa dyke ass acted like she didn't like me, but I didn't give a fuck shit she stole my bitch. I pulled up to the three-bedroom brick house and thought damn this could have been us but Cedes wanted to act fucking stupid dumb bitch. I got out and went straight to the door banging and ringing the doorbell like I was crazy as hell. Cedes came to the door with an attitude. Oh, this bitch must have thought I was some hoe ass nigga yeah, this bitch had definitely forgot the damage I used to do. I didn't even say shit I just started choking that bitch. Her eyes were wide, and she was scared. Yeah that is what I liked I kicked the door closed and kept choking her into the house. She was so damn pretty. I let her go and kissed her. I thought she was going to stop me, but she didn't she actually kissed me back yeah, she missed daddy. I grabbed the back of her hair and pulled her away from me. I kept my grip on her head and slapped her. "Ouch Hakeem damn what the fuck is your problem?" "Bitch what you tell Niya? You told her something about me?" I asked as I pushed to the ground. "What? No, I didn't! How the fuck did I tell her something and you was all over her. Did you tell her about your kids?" Cedes asked yeah that bitch was trying to test me. I crouched over her and said straight in her face "what kids?' She turned her head and looked away. I was done with her ass, I turned to leave but she called for me. "Keem" she sang in her sexy come fuck me voice. I turned around and she had lifted her shirt over those big 38D titties. Yes of course she still wanted Daddy and I was going to give her some of Daddy. After I fucked Cedes brains out it got me to wondering if she didn't tell Niya about us then where the fuck did the question come from? I hope Niya wasn't on no bullshit. Aniya I had been at Hakeem's house for three months and we still had not had sex. I was convinced he was sleeping with someone else. I mean did I not look good to him or something. He would be gone away from home until about six-thirty in the evening and yes, all day he would text me and make sure I was safe, but I wanted to know why we had not been intimate. Maybe he was disgusted by the situation with James. So many thoughts ran through my and I wanted to know and today was the day I was going to find out. I didn't have to work so I prepared a big meal for him. Cornbread, mashed potatoes, peas, Cornish hens, cabbage, and a peach cobbler, he was going to be well fed and well fucked. One thing my mother taught me was how to cook a meal. I made sure dinner was ready by six I got in the shower and dressed in some little shorts and a wife beater. I mean at the family dinner he addressed me as his woman and when we went out, he treated me like his woman. He had not made his move in sealing the deal, but I was willing to do it myself. I lit some candles on the cherry wood dining room table. Dinner was prepared and I was waiting for my man. He came home like clockwork. I heard the key turning in the lock and I was in the kitchen washing the last of the dishes. His sexy ass walked in the kitchen and I turned around and walked towards him. "Hey handsome, you ready to eat I cooked some good food for you." I said and kissed his lips just a peck. He looked happy and those hazel brown eyes sparkled. "Okay sexy let me get in the shower." He said and kissed me back. I melted. My short hair was curled I made sure I went to the shop to be fresh and cute. I had some lip gloss on my lips and a stop at Bath and Body Works had got my hygiene right. Yes, I was going to put this pussy on him. After fifteen minutes of waiting on the man I was getting impatient shit he still had to eat. But I had to be patient to make it extra special. He came into the kitchen with his pajama pants on a tee shirt. He looked at the food and was about to make his own plate. "No, no, no big daddy I got you today." I got up and grabbed a paper plate. "Damn you cook a meal like this and expect me to eat off a paper plate?" He asked and I could hear the disgust in his voice. "You right baby sorry," I said I had to make sure everything was perfect. That was probably why he hadn't given me any I was always fucking up. I mean what bitch would allow they man to eat off a paper plate that was some hood rat shit. This was not the first time he had to set me straight, but it was alright because he was just making sure I knew what he liked. He was only leading me into the right direction. I made his plate on the black round plate and made sure I warmed it up. Hakeem had gotten on me before that his food was not warm enough. I had to make sure I didn't make the same mistake twice. I sat down and we had a wonderful dinner.

We talked about everything I had discussed with him how I wanted to go to school to own my own boutique. He told me that I would be good at it and that he was one hundred percent behind me. I told him to go lay down while I cleaned the kitchen. That was another thing Hakeem did not like for me to cook and not clean the kitchen. One night I was too tired from work and didn't clean the kitchen and he was pissed. But he didn't yell at me or anything I just was on punishment I could not cook anything for an entire week. I loved cooking for him it made me feel useless when I couldn't do things for him. Once I got done with the kitchen, I was a bit buzzed from the wine that we had drank. I made my way to the back room. I walked in the room and stood over him. Hakeem was about 5' 10 and he had a built body. He was fine everything about him was perfect. He looked up at me and smiled. That smile those eyes I think I was in love. "What's up ma?" I straddled him, "I missed you." I said and kissed him. Not those damn pecks we usually do but I swallowed his tongue. He kissed me back and it definitely gave me the confidence to go ahead and give him all of me. I kissed him again, but I started from his lips to his neck, to his chest, and then I found my way to his dick. Yessss I had got a chance to touch it before and I tell you it was big. I smiled and licked my lips. I hadn't sucked dick in a while, and I was hoping that he would enjoy it. I put the tip in my mouth and just bopped my head a bit. Hakeem pushed my head down and I tried to take it all the way in, but he was too big. "Don't worry baby you don't have to put the whole thing just as much as you can" he said. Good cause I couldn't I licked his dick and pretended it was a Lollipop. He tasted so good and when I heard that moan, I knew that he was definitely loving the head. I stopped because I wanted to feel him. I took off my shirt and played with my nipples for him. I could tell he liked that. He grabbed my pants to pull them off. Once he got them off, he eased into me gently as he placed small kisses on my neck. "You feel so damn good girl," he whispered in my ear. "Oooh baby this dick so good" I moaned I had to admit Hakeem dick was good. Before I knew it there were tears falling from my eyes. He saw that I was crying and kissed the tears as he slowly but deeply made love to me. I knew at that moment I was in love. All night long he made love to me and I quietly fell in love as tears shed from all the pain, I had experienced. Hakeem really made me feel loved. The next morning Hakeem got up as usual. He kissed me good-bye as he left. I had to work that day and I tell you my head was everywhere but at the job. Hakeem was everything I needed at that moment I knew things were going to be okay. That was the feeling Hakeem gave me for some reason from the moment I met him. He was so fine I think I was blinded by his looks and not what I was really seeing an evil, hurt, scared little boy. I went to work with joy in my heart that day until I saw James. "Long time no see baby girl." He said as I looked up. He looked a mess, the clean-cut guy I was used to seeing was no more. I was convinced he was on that shit too. My heart skipped a beat and I know my damn heart was going to stop at any moment. I didn't say anything I just rang up the soda that he had and told him his total. "Oh, so you don't fucking hear me when I am talking to you? Well hear this if you don't come back to me, I will kill your mother." My eyes got wide. "Yup that's right you heard me bitch I will kill that bitch you hear me you belong to me." He threw the five-dollar bill at me and walked off without his change. I was in shock and I was scared. I asked my manager if I could go home early, I could not function like that. My hands were shaken, and I could tell he saw that I was uneasy. He asked me what had happened, but I was not about to tell him what was going on. I texted Hakeem and told him everything. He didn't respond. I was going crazy why he would want to hurt my mom, why hadn't he gotten over me, but most importantly why had Hakeem not answered my text? The incident had happened earlier that afternoon and here it was time for Hakeem to get off work and I had not heard anything from him. At this point, I had completely forgotten about my Mom shit she wasn't the best mother any fucking way. What I was worried about was why Hakeem had not come home yet it was seven thirty damn near eight o'clock and Hakeem had not made it. I had texted and called him with no answer, I was convinced he was with another chick. I was in the bed sleep when I heard him come in. I saw his silhouette in the dark as he grabbed some clothes. "Yeah you better wash that nasty bitch off you!" I yelled. He looked at me but didn't say anything. Ugh! I was pissed. He went and got in the shower and that definitely had pissed me off more. This dirty muthafucka couldn't even say anything to me he did not even care what I was going through. He came and got in the bed and grabbed me and tried to cuddle. "You got me fucked up I do not want your nasty ass touching me!" The tears were welling up in my eyes. "What the fuck are you crying for?" I guess he could hear the hurt in my voice. "Niya why the fuck you crying?" His voice was aggressive. "Because you cheating on me." I said really crying now. "Cheating on you, who said we were together?" That question made me feel stupid, I didn't have an answer, so I just shrugged my shoulders. He started laughing and I didn't find shit funny. I got up and went to the couch. He made me feel stupid I did not want to put up with his bullshit tonight. I was sleeping on the couch. The next morning Hakeem got up and went to work as usual. He was a jerk. He texted me throughout the day but since I was not his woman, I did not see the point in answering his texts. This was some bullshit I had given him myself we had made sweet love and now he told me I was not his woman. I needed to start saving so that I could move. I would have been moved but Hakeem would complain about how I looked, and I would take my money to fix myself up getting new clothes and underwear. But shit why should I be fixing myself up from someone and I wasn't their woman?

Chapter Six
HAKEEM

I was tired of that fuck nigga James fucking with my baby. When she texted me that shit, he said to her I left my work site immediately. My damn workers were asking me where I was going. I didn't have time to answer shit. I am the fucking boss I don't have to answer shit and I wasn't. I pulled up to the house but I didn't see James but that was okay I was going to wait for that hoe ass nigga. Two hours later and that nigga were still not at the house. Huh! I did not like to wait to kill a nigga. I started to pull off but then I thought about Niya crying wasn't no nigga gone make my bitch cry and that shit pissed me off more, so I stayed. I was parked across the street from the house so when James finally pulled up, I pulled off. I went around the block. I parked at the gas station around the corner from her Mama's house. My stupid ass was not thinking I had stayed parked out there too long. I know a neighbor, or something saw me. Just my luck the nigga must have needed something from the store because he pulled up at the gas station. That nigga parked at the gas pump next to me and got out. Dirty ass nigga didn't even lock his doors, good. I got in the back seat and crouched down. This shit was going to be easy. When James got in the car, he pulled off. I had the silencer on my pistol. When he pulled into the driveway, I sat up from my hiding spot. He was scared and confused but it was too late. I put the pistol to his head and put on bullet, in his brain. The glass shattering could be heard. I quickly hopped out of the car and ran through the yards back to the gas station. I was hoping like hell the camera didn't catch me, but I didn't have time to think about that. With all the crimes happening in Milwaukee shit nobody ever got caught and on top of that I knew somebody else had it out for James somewhere in the city. I kept texting Niya all day and this bitch was not answering any of my damn texts. I felt like going to whoop her ass, but I had too much shit going on with my business. This nigga Neil been fucking Steve's wife and they had a big ass brawl at one of the work site. I had to fill in for they stupid asses. I fired both those niggas I didn't give a fuck about that stupid shit. Niya had been blowing up my phone up that day that I had to kill James and instead of snapping out on her stupid ass I just ignored her. Shit as soon as I got home, she started talking shit. When she said I was cheating on her I felt bad for saying we weren't together, but she was pissing me the fuck off. I had just put the murder game down for your ungrateful ass and all you could do was bitch. She knew she was pissing me off not answering my text messages and shit. She better not had been giving that good pussy away. Man, I had been waiting all that time to give her some dick and I was cheating myself shit she had some good pussy. That shit was so tight and wet I couldn't do shit but fall in love with her ass. She was not going anywhere. She was crying and shit while we were having sex and I knew she had fallen in love. But right now, she was pissing me off not answering her damn phone. I felt like killing the bitch. It was damn near four in the afternoon and she was still not calling me back. Man, I was getting fucking mad. I had just done a job by myself and I could feel my asthma flaring up. My Mama had cursed me with that damn asthma "Fuck!" I said in between wheezing. I saw my asthma pump and picked it up and threw it out the window onto the street. I could make it to the hospital and by the time I made it there I would have a full fledge asthma attack that was going to teach Niya's ass not to answer for me.

ANIYA

It was about five in the evening when I got a call from Chiquita. She was hysterical on the phone. "Get to the Froedtert right now! Keemy is asking for you." She said into the phone. I didn't know what was going on or why Hakeem was in the hospital? I raced to Froedtert Hospital and they pointed me to the room that he was in. When I got in the room it was well lit and Hakeem had an oxygen mask over his face. He looked happy to see me. I didn't know what was going on. Chiquita had her head scarf on and was looking like a mother instead of a big sister. We hugged and I looked into her eyes for answers. "He's going to be okay he had an asthma attack. The doctor said he may have to go on steroids to help out, but he is okay." I looked at Hakeem and looked in confusion, "asthma attack I didn't know he had asthma." I said. Chiquita looked at her brother with an attitude. "That would explain why he had an asthma attack. He hasn't been taking his medication. He feels like it makes him weak because he has asthma ugh this boy here." I looked at Hakeem and walked over to him on the bed. I gave him a kiss on his forehead. "I'm sorry baby for stressing you out. I know you going to be okay I am going to take care of you." I meant every word I said. Hakeem was released a couple hours later, and I took him home. Chiquita was happy that he had someone to look over her baby brother and I was happy that I was some help. She gave me her number and told me to update her on his health and I reassured her I would. We stopped at CVS to pick up his medication. On our way home Hakeem apologized to me. "Niya I'm sorry I made you feel like you not my lady. You know I fuck with you and only you. But I don't think you ready to handle a nigga like me." "Why would you say that I been here I'm still here. I ain't going anywhere." I wanted him to know that we could get through anything. "Yeah you think I don't know but after I have done so much for you, you ready to leave me. I rescued you from your damn situation at home and all you can do is run your damn mouth nagging me and accusing me. I handled that situation with James that is why I didn't call you back. But no, as soon as I come home you all over a nigga, I don't need that type of stress. I know you trying to leave me and that's fucked up, but it is what it is. Then you thinking of ways to leave the nigga that's helping you leave then I hope you have a nice life." He turned and looked at the window. I felt so bad here I was ready to give up on the man so easily without even seeing his point of view. I was stupid and selfish. When we got home, I made dinner and we watched a movie. Later that night I went back to the room in the bed with my man. We made love and after we made love, I laid on his chest. I could hear the faint sound of a wheeze that I had never paid attention to before. "I love you Niya," Hakeem said to me and it took me by surprise. I looked up at him and his pretty brown eyes were so beautiful, so inviting, so loving. "I love you too baby." I kissed his lips. Yes, I loved that man that man Hakeem who had treated me like a queen. Yes, that's what they do build you up to break you down. I had not known it then, but I know it now.

Chapter Seven

HAKEEM

We had been dating for about two years when Niya became pregnant with our son Malcolm. Things had been going good for us I had more clients with my cleaning company, and I was ready to start a family. I came home from work and Niya's lazy ass was laying in the bed and I had not smelt no good cooking. We had been trying for six months to get pregnant and I was getting mad. That bitch Cedes was popping kids fast as hell when we were together. "What you doing laying down you didn't make me anything to eat?" I asked her. Shit I was taking care of her ass the least she could do was make sure I ate. I had started making her put all her work checks in my bank account so that I could control the money. I gave her ass a weekly allowance of what I felt like she needed. I had put her name on the account, and she didn't even know; and I wasn't gone tell her ass neither. "Babe I do not feel good I think I may be pregnant," She groaned. I was excited shit about time. "Okay let me run to the store and get you a test." I ran my ass to the store so quick and came back finally she was pregnant. I came back in less than five minutes and made her go pee on the stick. We were going to have a baby. She came back with that stupid ass stick with one fucking line and that shit pissed me the fuck off!   "What the fuck man! Can you have kids? That nigga James probably fucked you up shit you so fucking nasty letting that nigga fuck on you knowing he was fucking your Mama! Nasty ass bitch!" Man, she was stupid as hell for letting that nigga fuck on her she knew what she was doing. "Fuck you! How the fuck I don't know it ain't your nasty ass that gave me something shit! Leaving the house all times of the day like you at work, you not working that many damn hours!" As soon as the sentence left her mouth, I slapped the shit out of her in her mouth. I hit her ass fast and hard. She grabbed her face and ran to the room. I didn't give a fuck about her ass crying I had given her too many passes with that slick ass mouth she was going to learn. I came into the room and got behind her and kissed her neck. She was fucking hysterical crying. The shit wasn't even that serious I had only slapped her ass damn she was acting like I had killed her ass. "I'm sorry Niya but you need to watch your mouth." I kissed her neck again and wrapped my arms around her waist. She didn't say anything, so I kissed and rubbed all over her soft body damn I wanted her to have my baby "I never hit you before and I promise I won't do it again, I love you." She turned around and looked at me. I had tears in my eyes not because I was sad about hitting her but because I wanted her to be with me all the time, I loved her so damn much. She forgave me that night and every other night and day for the next five years. Every time I would hit her, hurt her, and cuss her out she would forgive me because she loved me, I provided for her, I was going to be her baby's daddy. And that night as I planted my seeds down deep inside Niya she became pregnant and I was happy as fuck. We had planned this baby and I wanted a baby. That is until I found out I was having a boy. Aniya That first time that Hakeem had slapped me I didn't even know what to do. I was hurt behind the shit for real. He hugged me and rubbed me all night long and kissed me and told me how much he loved me. Those tears he was crying was just enough to push me over the edge I loved this guy and he loved me he didn't mean to hurt me. I know it was that first time he hit me that I got pregnant with Malcolm. Hakeem was so excited he wanted us to be a family and although I could still feel the pain from the slap across my face, I had too much love in my heart for the man. I knew he loved me and wanted this baby but when it came time to see what we were having I guess Hakeem decided he did not want any parts because it was a boy. As soon as we left the ultrasound from finding out what we were having Hakeem tore into me. "What the fuck you must have been fucking some other nigga I can't have boys." He said to me. That shit just sounded stupid. I was highly irritated and putting up with his stupidity today was not an option. "Hakeem you don't have any kids so you don't know what you can have. And plus, you get what God blesses you with." I rolled my eyes. "Bitch God ain't got nothing to do with you being a hoe. First we couldn't get pregnant I find this shit fishy something ain't right." Ugh he had never expressed doubts before so now he trying to say this dumb ass shit. "Hakeem you are the father we can get a DNA test and everything, but this is your baby boy or girl it's yours!" I screamed at him he was getting on my damn nerves. "Bitch who the fuck is your stupid ass yelling at I got something for your ass when we get home." He parked in the driveway and I got out the car. I was not worried about his ass he had not hit me since that day when the pregnancy test was negative, so the thought never came in my head. Plus, I was pregnant with his child he was not going to hit me I thought but I was wrong. I went to lie down and he jumped on my ass. He jumped on top of me and started choking me. He was on my stomach and I could not breathe. I was like a fish caught out of water. I could feel my body losing consciousness. He was choking me so hard and long I couldn't do anything but lay there because he was sitting on top of me. I wanted to scream, and I wanted to cry but I couldn't I was thinking about how did I get myself into this situation. He was ready to kill me and my unborn son. That was the last thing I remembered before I blacked out. I was awakened to cold water being thrown on me. I thought I was drowning. I immediately grasped for air. When he saw that I was up he came over to me. I put my hands over my stomach just to protect my unborn son. If he would choke me unconscious, then what would he do to the baby in my stomach my mind started wheeling with evil thoughts of this man. "Damn I thought you were dead. Don't do that shit to me no more girl." He said kissing me. "You gotta watch your damn mouth girl you make me lose my damn mind." He walked out of the room and grabbed me a towel. I was in pure shock I really didn't know what had happened. No, I knew what happened, but it had not registered clearly because Hakeem was acting like I had done something wrong. My mind was racing, and I couldn't think straight had I done something wrong? I sat up and was kind of dizzy. "I think I need to go to the hospital." I said feeling really weak. "And what you gone tell them when you get there you trying to get me locked up Niya!" He was looking scared. "What? No, I need to make sure the baby is okay." I really was not thinking about calling the police I was really concerned about the baby. "He okay it's not like you quit breathing or anything. You just fell asleep while I was on top of you," he made it seem like it was the truth. He was a crazy muthafucka. "While you were on top of me while you was choking me, I went unconscious." He started laughing and I was confused why the hell was he laughing this shit was not a joke. He was pissing me off and I needed to get out of there. "Choking you? Girl I was not choking you I was on top of you kissing you and I guess you fell asleep. I think you just tired from all the stress of you finding out the baby is a boy and not mine." He grabbed my arm and I flinched. "What's wrong baby?" He knew what was wrong he knew he had choked me, but he wanted me to feel like I was crazy like I had not just gotten choked. I didn't even care about him saying the baby wasn't his. I could still feel the pressure of his hands around my neck. He made me lay back down. He thought I was just going to go to sleep without making sure my son was okay. I let him go to sleep and I tiptoed my way out of the house. I went to the hospital to make sure my baby was okay. I was crying and in so much pain I didn't know what to do. I was not physically in pain, but the mental pain was too much to bear. I was in denial of everything that was going on, but the truth of the matter was it seemed to me like Hakeem was abusive. While I was getting the ultrasound and listening to my baby boy's heartbeat, I called Chiquita Hakeem's sister. She seemed worried about me and I told her where I was but to not tell Hakeem. The doctor's said my blood pressure was up so they were going to keep me for observations to make sure it would go down.

Chapter Eight
HAKEEM

The sound of the phone ringing brought me out of my sleep. I looked and saw it was my big sister, so I definitely was going to answer. She was my world and her calling me late at night I was hoping that I didn't have to fuck anybody up. "Hello!" She screamed into the phone. "Quita what's wrong?" I sat straight up something was definitely wrong I could hear it in her voice. "Niya she at Froedtert hospital." I looked at my phone cause I knew I had heard her wrong. I turned over to find the empty space in the bed. I know this bitch didn't. I got up and got dressed in two minutes. I don't know if Quita was still on the phone or what, but I needed to get to the hospital. After I got on some clothes I headed to the car. As I started up my Camaro, I dialed Quita's number. "What room number?" "I don't know they not giving me no information." She complained. Dammit that mean the bitch had to tell them something for them to not want to give out the room number. Shit! She better not had told them anything. I was going to the hospital just so if she did then I would not look suspicious. When I got to the hospital, I guess the nurses had finally given Quita the room number because she said that she had it. Good I could get my ass in that room and see what was up. I was going to beat her ass if she told them what really happened. I told her ass not to be coming up to the damn hospital. I wanted to beat her ass all over again. Quita fat ass was out of breath as we power walked to the room. When we got to the room she was sleep. I stood over her watching her sleep. She was so beautiful just like an angel. She stirred and opened her eyes and looked dead at me. She had the look of terror and it made me feel like shit. I didn't want her to feel scared of me. She just needed to watch how she talked to her man. "Girl they were acting like they didn't want to give me your room number." Quita said loudly. "So, what they say about the baby?" "They said he is okay, but my blood pressure is up, they want to make sure I am okay." She explained to Quita but was looking at me.

Damn I wanted to ask her about the cops but shit then I would be admitting I choked her ass and I was not going to do that. "Hakeem told me what happened and yes he was wrong," Quita slapped me upside my head, "I do not know what would possess him to say this baby ain't his but he wrong ain't you boy?" I hadn't told Quita shit, but my sister knew what was up and she was helping me out. I gave Niya the saddest puppy dog eyes I could muster up. Yeah, I knew the baby was mine but why the fuck did I keep having boys. I was cursed I didn't want any boys because I didn't want the same hate my father had against me to build up against my sons. That was the real reason I really did not bother Cedes because I didn't want the kids, so it wasn't no reason for me to keep her around. "I am sorry baby I am just scared to have a baby, but I know that we will be great parents." I said and kissed her on the forehead. I was wrong and I needed to try and do right by Niya. "Baby we in this together," she told me, "you know I am not going anywhere I just needed to make sure the baby was okay." When she said that I felt so much better yes, she was still my lady and I had a chance to do right by her and I was not trying to fuck it up. Aniya Chiquita had decided to throw me a baby shower which I thought was stupid since I did not have many friends. I invited Mya and I called my mother for the first time in two years to invite her. I missed my mother and she didn't even know she was having a grandchild. I didn't get an answer from her, so I decided to stop by her house one afternoon. We didn't have the perfect relationship, but she was my Mother and I loved her even with her flaws. I was eight months pregnant and it was a week before the baby shower and I still could not get in touch with my mother I was sincerely worried about her. I pulled up at the house and I didn't see her car. I knocked on the door and didn't get an answer. I put my key in the lock and it still worked. The house was dark all the furniture in the living room and kitchen was gone and it looked like no one lived there. I heard water running in the bathroom and I went and knocked on the door. "Mommy are you in there?" I asked knocking on the door damn I hoped James was not in there. What was I thinking going in the house without Hakeem. I was eight months pregnant I could not defend myself if he attacked me. But something inside was telling me I was going to be okay. I still heard the water running and that alarmed me. I turned the knob and it wasn't locked. I walked in the bathroom and my heart sank to my feet. There was my mother in the tub unconscious, with slit writs blood and water was everywhere. I screamed.

"No! No! Mommy get up!" I ran across the bathroom like I was not eight months pregnant. The lord had to be with me since there was so much water on the floor, but I did not slip or fall. I kneeled next to the tub. I checked her pulse, nothing. My heart sank into the pit of my stomach. I wanted to let out a gut-wrenching scream, but I couldn't I was to hurt. My mother and I didn't get along, but she was my mother. I called Hakeem he answered on the first ring. I was hysterical. I had to calm down he was could not understand me. I took three deep breaths. One, two, three I stammered and stuttered my mama, my mama. He said he was on his way but how could he be on his way and he didn't know where I was. But ten minutes later Hakeem was coming through the door rescuing me. I was still holding my mother crying I didn't know what to do. I didn't have any siblings or a father all I had was her and although she didn't treat me so good and she didn't protect me she was all I had and now I didn't even have her. "What the fuck! Niya baby get up!" I could hear the tears in his voice. I snapped back to reality this man had lost his mother also and here I was calling him to save me. What was I thinking I needed to call the ambulance? Hakeem must have been thinking the same thing because he called the ambulance before I could. I will never forget that day the day my mother died it was October 6 and I had Malcolm November 6. I could never forget that pain I felt the lost I felt. I had to go on bed rest after that. I was so close to going into preterm labor. I had missed my baby shower but Hakeem he was so great the entire time. He cried with me, he held me, and he made me feel like I would be okay because he knew I was alone. Well I had him and his sisters and baby Malcolm now. But with all good things come the bad, and it seemed like those were the best times between Hakeem and I because over the next couple of years he dogged me out. It was like I was trapped, and he knew it. I had no mother, no father, nothing just him and he used that to his advantage.

Chapter Nine
HAKEEM

When Niya's mother died she left her the sole beneficiary and she got 100 thousand dollars. I was happy as fuck I used that money to start another business of carpentry. I didn't know shit about carpentry, but my nigga Lance knew everything, so I let him run it. The rest of the money I used to buy a home and remodel it and flip it. That was what a nigga really wanted to do rehabilitate homes and because of Niya I was able to do it. She just didn't know how happy that made me. I had damn near fifty thousand dollars to my name in my bank account. I still had Niya on the account, but she didn't know. I also put her on my insurance policy so that if anything happened her and my son would be good. My sister Quita kept trying to make me put it in her name but fuck that if anything happened to me while at work then my kids needed to be taken care of. I wasn't stupid I owned everything and took care of everything and I was not about to leave Aniya assed out. She had my kids and at the end of day she deserved it all. I made sure her names were on all my companies she was my everything and I wanted to make sure she was straight if anything happened to me. She had given me the entire check without any hesitation, and I appreciated that. I made sure she quit working at punk ass Wal-Mart and I fully took care of her. That was the least I could do this girl had invested in me and that shit just made me love her more. Although I loved the fuck out of the girl, she always knew a way to fuck it up. I gave her ass two hundred dollars every week to spend on what she needed. Shit I was getting dough now, but the goal was to save. We had moved to a bigger apartment that was two bedrooms and we had a dining room, living room, it was nice enough. We had eaten dinner and she went to lie our son Malcolm in his bed. I wasn't too fond of the little nigga but I took care of him so that was enough. Shit I had three other sons that I wasn't taking care of so I thought that was the least I could do because I really did love Niya. She was my everything and because of that I accepted our son, but I wasn't about to play with the little nigga. He was handsome too and looked just like me and that really made me steer clear of his ass. I would catch his gray eyes staring a hole in me sometimes. She came into the room where I was and started ironing my clothes. The way her ass looked in that gown was making my dick hard. I was about to give her some dick, but she fucked that up by opening her fucking mouth. "Baby I still have some money for like gas and stuff, but I need some more money." She said "For what?" I growled I wasn't trying to be mean but shit she knew I was trying to save. "Nothing never mind." She whispered but I detected a little fucking attitude. Oh, this bitch wants to act stupid because I asked her ass what she needed the money for. Shit she talking about nothing bitch you need the money for something. I got up and grabbed her from behind and started choking her "Bitch you getting on my muthafucking nerves." I was choking the shit out of her. I knew she wasn't really scared, or she would have just answered my question and not gave me attitude. I threw her ass on the bed. She was trying to catch her breath. I walked up on her and punched her dead in her fucking eye. Stupid bitch should have been trying to worry about why the fuck I am mad instead of catching her breath. "Bitch shut the fuck up!" I screamed and then the little muthafucking bastard wanted to get to crying "And get that got damn baby before I beat his ass too!" Shit I didn't want to hear that shit I had a hard day juggling three different work sites and shit I did not want no fucking back talk. I was tired after beating her ass that I fell asleep. I woke up at two in the morning and felt that Niya was not in the bed with me. I got up and found her in the bed with the baby. There was a little twin-size bed in his room. I shook her awake I wanted her next to me. She looked at me with those beautiful hazel eyes and I knew she was hurting "I think the baby is getting a little sick baby I will just watch him for a little while longer," she yawned. I didn't even say anything because I saw that her eye was black and felt bad as hell. I knew she would get back in the bed with me when she was ready and the way that I had hit her in her eye I knew that she was a bit mad. But she was going to have to learn not to talk back to her man.

ANIYA

I decided to get Malcolm and take him to the park we were going to play hooky today. It was a nice summer day thank God since I had to wear my big sunglasses. The kids were out of school, so I got to see all the other kids at the playground. They were beautiful I loved children. I put Malcolm in the swing and swung him. He was such a happy baby. I loved that about him. The sun was causing me to get a little dizzy, so I decided to sit down. Malcolm seemed a bit tired, so I rocked him to sleep and laid him in his stroller. I was in deep thought when I heard a voice. I looked up and there was Cedes. "Hey stranger, how are you?" She asked and it seemed as if she was looking through my glasses. "I'm good and you?" I scooted over so that she could sit on the left of me, but she insisted on sitting on the right of me. The bitch was irritating me. "I am fabulous honey. Is that the baby?" She looked at Malcolm I shook my head. "Oh, he is beautiful looks just like his father." She said smiling. We sat in an awkward silence for a moment. "So how is Hakeem liking fatherhood?" She asked. "Oh, he is fine," I lied, "he buys things for him every week he did a marvelous job on his bedroom, we are going to get him a play set this week sometime whenever he gets time off work. You know he stays busy since he expanded his business. Yup he is excellent." I was lying like fuck, but I was not about to let this bitch know that I was miserable hell I really did not even know her. She just looked at me and smiled. "That is terrific honey I am glad that he takes care of his responsibility." She got up and starting playing with her kids and I was happy about that. Her three boys were big. And they must have looked like their daddy because they were light skinned with curly hair, cute kids. Before I left the park, I walked up to Cedes to say good-bye hell she had never done anything bad to me. As I approached her, I noticed the scar on her face. It was a deep gash that I had not noticed before, she was still pretty but it was disturbing. "I just wanted to say bye before I left." I said she grabbed me and hugged me, I wasn't gay, and I hope she didn't think I was. I heard her whisper a prayer. Heavenly father give this woman the strength, the courage, and the things she need to guide her through life Amen. She let me go and she walked away I didn't know what that was about but somehow, I needed that it made me feel good. Later that night Hakeem and I cuddled up watching movies. I loved the way his soap smelled on his body. We used the same Zest, but it was something about the way it smelled on my man that just did things to me. I loved this man and the way he wrapped his hands around me made me feel so secure and safe. Ain't that strange he was the one hurting me, but he was also the one who made me feel safe. Life can be fucked up like that sometimes have your ass damn near loony. "How was your day?" "It was good." I said and it had been good. "Yeah u needed a break from school." He said damn how had he known I wasn't at school. "Yeah try to clear my mind and spend some time with Malcolm." "So yesterday when you said never mind what did you need baby. You know I don't like when you don't tell me what you need." "Oh, I just wanted to buy Malcolm a play set that's all." I said with tears in my eyes why our conversation could not be this simple yesterday. It takes for him to beat my ass for us to have a civilized conversation was this relationship was coming too that shit was not even right. "Oh, okay babe we can go tomorrow and go look at some toys for my little man." He said. He always claimed him when he was in a good mood. But he would deny him with the next breath. Malcolm was his splitting fucking image so I do not know why he would deny his son. I loved going to school. It was my relief and I was pretty smart. I had started my business classes and I planned on going for the next four years I wanted to be just like Hakeem he was my role model. He was very smart and very successful. I made my way to class that Monday morning and I felt good. Although I still had my black eye Hakeem and I had made up, so I felt better. I sat in my economics class and my teacher stared at me. "Niya you are going to have to take those sunglasses off in my class." She said. I had went through the entire day without my other instructors saying anything to me. So, what was her beef? "I can't." I had makeup on, but you could still see the swelling on my face. "Well you will just have to leave my class." I looked around at the other students why was she doing this to me? I got up and stormed out of the classroom. I was in tears by the time I reached my car. Why did she have to embarrass me like that? She was wrong she knew something was wrong so why couldn't she just let it be. Over the next years I would have to endure the pain of people seeing me bruised up. That was the first time he had blackened my eye, but it wasn't the last. In order for me to finish my degree I had to accept the fact that I was getting beaten on. So, I came to school with busted lips, black eyes, and scars that you could see because my skin was so light. I was embarrassed at first but after a while I got over it. Hell, I was trying to better my life for me and my son at that time, so I didn't care what anyone thought. Plus, who was they to judge my man was taking care of me. I called Mya to see if she wanted to go out for a late lunch, I needed somebody to talk to. She was my only friend and although I didn't tell her about everything that went on in my life, I still told her bits and pieces of how

Hakeem wasn't claiming Malcolm sometimes but that was it. The beatings I kept to myself. She said that she couldn't make it, so I decided to go ahead and go to Applebee's by myself. I saw a purple truck in the parking lot, and it looked a lot like Hakeem's, but he was at work and plus purple Cadillac Escalades were everywhere. I made sure my hair was on point and I put some pink lipstick on my full lips. I had on a blue colorful halter top that hugged my titties just right. The white long skirt that I had on was cool, but it was still too warm for it. Thank goodness for air conditioning. I got to the entrance and I looked in through the window and saw Hakeem with a dark-skinned chick. I stormed right in past the hostess. Everybody was looking at me like I was crazy, and I was. This nigga had told me he was at work but here he was sitting having lunch with some hoe. And here I was missing school because he had blacked my eye oh no, he had me fucked up. I walked right up to the table and he was so engaged in talking he didn't even notice me standing there. "Damn did work let out early?" I asked as calmly as possible. He looked up at me in shock. The lady was sitting there smirking like she thought something was funny. The bitch wasn't even cute. She had long pretty hair, but her facial features were ugly her nose was too big for her face and her eyes was small, so she looked cross eyes. "And you here with this ugly bitch." That made her mad her smirk turned into a frown. She stood up. "Who the fuck you calling ugly you fat bitch!" She yelled that's when Hakeem got up. "Bitch you not about to sit here and disrespect my baby mama like that." I was shocked and so was she. Here he was on a lunch date with the bitch, but he was taking up for me. That's the stupid shit niggas do. Disrespect you for these trash ass hoes. "Fuck the both of yall!" I yelled and punched her in her fucking face because she was still smirking, and it was pissing me off more. I did know how to fight, and I was tagging that ass. I punched her in her face, and she tried to grab for me I jumped back and jumped forward and did a one two combo on that ass. Yea for a big bitch I could stick and move. She fell on the floor and I jumped on top of her and started swinging. Somebody said they were calling the police and Hakeem grabbed me and we left. "Get the fuck off me Hakeem!" I screamed when I got out the restaurant. "You putting me through all this shit and fucking another bitch." My glasses had fallen off by now and I didn't know where they were. Here I was with a black eye and fighting for this nigga to prove my love I felt stupid as hell. "Calm down baby just calm down." He tried to reach for me. "Nope fuck that I am leaving you fuck you!" I screamed. "Okay Niya with what money?" He asked. And I sat there in silence and feeling stupid. But I had a comeback for him. "I will sell my car. I know I can get a couple of thousands." I stormed off to my car and got in. Hakeem was standing there looking at me. He told me to rise down my window and I did. He pulled out a wad of cash. "Here Niya you ain't gotta sell your car if you wanna leave then leave I got you." He walked off. Damn was it that easy for him to let me walk out on him like that. Shit he didn't even want me. I watched as he got in his car and I found my other pair of sunglasses. The tears were flowing, and I was ready to get out of there. The nigga didn't even want me.

Chapter Ten
HAKEEM

The day that Niya saw Sylvia and I at Applebee's and fought that girl man I was hurt behind it. Sylvia was on some bullshit because I hadn't been fucking with her like that. I was still fucking her from time to time, but she wanted more. We were only at Applebee's because she told me that if I did not come, she would tell Niya about us. How ironic Niya came in that day. Hell, nah I didn't want her to leave me but the look on her face when she was fighting, the look on her face when I had hit her, that damn black eye I just didn't want her to hurt and I felt like if she left then we might be better off. I didn't want to hurt my baby but that was all I knew. I had tried to talk to Quita about our fights, but my damn sister condoned everything I did like it was right. Niya had moved her and Malcolm into a one-bedroom apartment and I paid for everything. I wanted my baby to know that I loved her. I even missed Malcolm little crybaby ass the nigga was the spitting image of me, and I did care about him. I didn't want to hurt him, and I didn't want to hurt her now I was alone. I was lying in my empty ass bed thinking about Niya's pretty face when my phone rung and I saw that it was my baby girl. I smiled any chance I got to talk to her I was happy I tried not press her, but I really did miss her. "Hey babe." I cooed in the phone. "Hey honey are you really busy today?" "No not too much sweetheart what's wrong?" "Well I have an exam and Malcolm's daycare is not open and I need someone to keep him." She said. "Shit he can ride with me I am his daddy. You at home?" Shit that little nigga could kick it with me while I made my rounds to my workers. "Yeah I am." She said happily. "Okay I will be there in a minute I wanted to talk to you anyway," I jumped up and was at her damn house in five minutes. She came to the car with a happy Malcolm and his baby bag. I got out and helped her put him in the car. I really didn't know what the fuck I was doing but I was going to make it look good. "I told you I needed to talk to you." She jumped into the passenger side of my truck. She looked good as fuck and she smelled good like some damn flowers. I was looking fucked up I know my damn curly hair had grown out and my beard was long and grown out. "I know you gotta be at school, but I just wanted to know when you coming back home?" I was not about to beat around the bush I needed her ass back. I missed rubbing her thick, soft thighs at night. "I know we had our problems babe, but everything is going to be different we going to get back right." "I know baby I am so ready to come back home it don't make no sense." She confessed. That had a nigga smiling from ear to ear my baby missed me and that shit made me feel good. I dropped her off at school and took my little man on a ride with me. He was a cool little fella and I had to admit that he reminded me a lot of myself. Aniya I moved back in at the end of the month and Hakeem took care of everything. We settled back in nicely. And I must admit Hakeem had even started helping me with Malcolm more. He loved the fact that our baby was crawling and about to start walking. He taught him how to walk before his first birthday. He had put so much time and effort into winning me back that I never thought that things would go back to being the same. It took for him to cheat on me for me to leave but I never left when he hit me. He probably had other women after that chick, but I never knew about any of them. I was too busy worrying about other things. We decided to have cake and ice cream at the house for Malcolm's first birthday. Vanessa and Cedes brought over some gifts for Malcolm and Chiquita bought him one of those battery-operated cars, they spoiled him. I tried to see if Mya was coming but I couldn't reach her. She had been kind of distant since I had moved back in with Hakeem. I think she was a little jealous because after years of tolerating Chris ass he had left her for some other woman whom he had gotten pregnant. I think it really hurt Mya because they had been trying for years to have a baby and BAM one day Chris walks in and tells her he had a baby on the way. At first Mya tried to be okay with it. The truth was Chris didn't think Mya was good enough for him since she couldn't get pregnant. Yes, men loved their baby mamas. I was living proof of that. I am sure Hakeem had other bitches that he talked too and even had sex with but nothing else mattered but Malcolm and I. Everything went together just like chicken and macaroni. We were the perfect couple and I loved my man everyday was a dream with the occasional fighting. I can't lie I really was tired of the shit, but it is like when you love a man they are like a drug. People always act like alcohol, weed, and coke are the only things that you can be addicted too. Fall in love with the devil and see how easy you can leave him. Hakeem got me addicted to him in so many ways that I didn't even know that he was getting me. You know now that I think back on it, I wasn't addicted but more of attached, dependent. Just think I didn't have any money the only money I had was whatever he gave me. I had bought me a new convertible Porsche when I got that money from my Mother but that was it, I gave the rest of the money to Hakeem to expand his business. That was where I had fucked up the most. Next I had fucked up when I first met him and told him my entire business yes, I was in a fucked-up situation, but I should have been smart and went to a professional. Sometimes when we would get into it, he would make it very clear all that he did for me. "Bitch I took you in" and "yo mama didn't give a fuck about you" the damn list went on and on how he would break me down. I think that the words hurt more than the physical abuse. Over the years the abuse got worse. There was a point where Malcolm was three years old and Hakeem had blackened both my eyes, I had a bruised rib from where he kicked me. I had so many scars in the inside that my beautiful face didn't mean anything. Every time I looked at my face all I saw was that black eye, or that busted lip even after it had healed. I was a broken woman and he knew it. He used that against me so much that you would be surprised that I was still alive. Yes, I had survived, and Hakeem had not. Now here I was sitting on the bus riding to the insurance company to see what my dead baby daddy had for me. Every time I closed my eyes could still see his lifeless face when the ambulance came. He was still Hakeem, but he wasn't moving, and his face was in shock. I still remember how he looked when he was in the casket. I cried although I was relieved, I was still hurt. Hell, he was the father of my children and I still loved him. Malcolm seemed okay with the fact that his father was dead. He understood more than I wanted him too. Deena was still young, and I don't think she realized that she had lost her father.

Chapter Eleven

ANIYA

Malcolm was three when I got pregnant with Deena and yes, we planned her also. I had stopped taking my birth control pills and just like a stupid ass I got myself pregnant with another one of his kids. It wasn't as hard as with Malcolm, yet this pregnancy was different. The entire time I was pregnant with Deena it was horrible. I threw up from day one I had heart burn it was like I was pregnant with a little demon. It was horrible and I knew that I was in for something serious. I was in pain and Hakeem was happy. I had to quit school because I could not do it. I was surprised that he was helping so much with Malcolm. He would take him to daycare during the day so that I could be alone. Hell, I was miserable, so the alone part was not even helpful. I would get up early and throw up as soon as the clock hit six o'clock. Then everything I ate would taste like chalk, but I had to eat. And through the entire pregnancy Hakeem did not hit me. He was too happy that we were having a girl. The day we went to see what we were having you would have thought they told him he won a million dollars. The lady had to keep telling him over and over. He took me shopping every week and he cooked dinner. He wanted to make sure my food intake was good since I was so sick. I didn't even know Hakeem knew how to cook he had never cooked since we had been together. Yes, life was great with the occasional arguing, but it was like Hakeem was a changed man. Even if I got an attitude with him, he just blamed it on the pregnancy. Not like with Malcolm oh no if I was to talk back or be disrespectful when I was pregnant with Malcolm my ass would have gotten beat but nope not with A'Deena. A'Deena was Hakeem's mother name so we decided to name her after his deceased mother. We had already named our son after his father Malcolm. I really wanted to name our daughter after my mother but when I brought up that idea that was the one time, I thought I was going to get my ass beat. We were sitting in the kitchen and Malcolm was playing with his toys in the living room.

He was such a good boy he listened well, and he wasn't a crier ever since he had become older. I was eating some soup and Hakeem was eating the chicken and spaghetti he made for him and Malcolm. Damn all these years I had been cooking I thought he didn't know how to cook because he would throw a tantrum if I didn't have the food ready. And hell, from the smell of it he knew how to cook better than me. Having food ready for him was just one of his many ways of controlling me. "Baby I wanted to talk about baby names; I think we should name the baby after my mother." I said and I wish I hadn't said that. Hakeem was wearing a white shirt and some of the spaghetti sauce spilled on it because he was in utter shock that I had said that. He was dramatic like that if I said something that he didn't agree with his whole face would show his disapproval. "What is our son's name?" He asked. I wanted to ask him what the fuck did that have to do with anything, but he didn't allow me to respond. "Bitch is you stupid! What the fuck is our son's name!" "Malcolm!" I yelled back this muthafucka was crazy. "Yes, Malcolm. Malcolm is my father's name so it would only be right that we name our daughter after my mother. My father and mother lived together do you know your father?" He got up and was in my face. I didn't say anything tears were streaming down my face now. He knew how I felt about not knowing my father. "Do you know your father!" He yelled again. "No." I cried through my tears. "Why the fuck is you crying Niya? I am asking you a simple question. You so fucking soft." He muffed my head. "Listen to me and listen to me good. I know you love your mother but your mother ain't shit. She let niggas rape you, do you really want to name our daughter after someone who would do that to their own child." I didn't say anything because in so many ways he was right, but she was still my mother. "Bitch you so stupid that's your damn problem you think everybody is stupid like you. You want to make a fucking mockery of me and my kids bitch!" "No Hakeem just forget it," I said and tried to get up, but he made me sit back down. "Naw you wanna say stupid shit so you gone sit here and listen to what the fuck I gotta say. Saying that stupid shit like it's okay. Naw bitch it's not okay." By this time Malcolm had stopped playing and was looking and listening to his father. I hated when Hakeem belittled me in front of our son. Allowing Hakeem to disrespect my son was only an open river to allow my son to disrespect women. And the older he got the more he clung onto his daddy's every word. Hakeem still did not play with Malcolm and love him as much as he should, but the boy loved his father. He always said things like Daddy gone be mad Niya or Daddy don't tolerate that. Yes, a three-year-old already knew who obeyed who. I was living in shame and sometimes I thought that it was okay but most of the time it upset me. Here I was a grown woman letting my "man" talk to me like I was a little kid. I had more sense than that or did I? My mother had never really taught me how to approach men or behave around men. Lisa was my mother and she was a beautiful woman. So beautiful I was happy to look just like her. I remember as early as I could that people would always say "you look just like your mama." Yes, that was a blessing to be light skinned damn near white. Neither one of us had real long hair but Mama always wore a wig she made sure my short hair was cute and styled. Yes, looking like my mother was a blessing and a curse I learned that early on in life. Just because I was a young girl that didn't stop the men from wanting me, the sick ones looked at me as if I was a grown woman. That is what Mr. Jones thought of me. Mr. Jones was one of mother's male friends she dated when I was younger. He was a tall, fat, light skinned man who smelled like sweat. He would come by our house in all his fancy outfits and nice cars. He showered Mama's fine ass that is what he called her with all types of gifts. He even bought me pretty dresses. One day Mama was gone with her other male friend William, see Mother had many male friends. William was her favorite guy though. Whenever he would call, she would drop everything and get really pretty in those clothes Mr. Jones had bought and leave. It did not matter that I didn't have a babysitter I could watch myself. Yes, at seven years old I was watching myself. This particular night William had called Mama and she had ran off to be with him. My guess is that she didn't let Mr. Jones know that she would be gone so he came knocking on our door that night. I knew Mr. Jones so I let him in. He was mad when I told him that mama had left with William, I thought he knew about William, but I guess he didn't. He looked at me in my princess gown and I felt funny. "Come here Niya and sit on my lap," he said, and I did he was a nice man there was no reason for me to be afraid. I sat on his lap and I felt something under my butt, and I jumped up. "Don't be afraid Niya it is okay." I climbed back on his lap really slowly. Mr. Jones started hugging me and it felt good. I didn't have a father and my Mother never hugged me it felt nice to feel loved. That is what I felt like Mr. Jones was trying to be a father to me. He kissed me on my forehead while he was rubbing my leg. But he was getting close to my private area. "Don't be afraid Niya

I just want to touch it." His breathing was heavy, and I was scared. I opened up my legs and let him rub, on my pussy. I didn't know it was a bad thing it didn't really feel bad until I felt the wetness. Mama had not taught me to not let a man touch on me down there. Plus, Mama let men touch her down there. As Mother's things that we do in front of our kids we shouldn't do. Kids are like sponges they soak everything up. So here I was seven years old letting Mr. Jones play with my pussy. But that was all he did was touch me down there and put his finger in me. Mr. Jones was an okay man I thought. He still came by to see Mama and he still bought me things too. And when Mama wasn't at home, he came to visit me, and we played the touchy feely game.

Chapter Twelve
ANIYA

r. Jones had been molesting me for about five months before Mama found out. It was one day when she noticed that Mr. Jones had left his wallet at our house. I hadn't been seeing Mr. Jones during the day anymore, only at night when he came to "babysit" me. "Niya has Mr. Jones been over here?" I looked at her crazy. Of course, Mr. Jones had been over here, he told me that she said that he could start babysitting me after that first night she had left me alone. "Duh Mama," I said. "Duh Mama what you saying Niya I didn't know Mr. Jones had been over here." She said her light face turned red and I knew she was angry. "Mama he has been babysitting me." I said and I thought my mother was going to pass out the way she put her hand over her chest. "Niya come here baby." I came to my mother she was sitting on the floor of the bathroom. "Has Mr. Jones been touching on you?" "Yes, Mama we play the touchy-feely game and he touches my private area." I confessed I didn't know that it was a bad thing I thought that she knew. He told me that my mama was okay with it and that she wanted me to let him to touch me because that was a part of babysitting. She had never told me that letting someone touch me down there was a bad thing. My mother started crying. "Baby you don't let anyone touch you down there ever again." She cried. I never saw Mr. Jones after that but Mama never had to work after that until the day he died. I always say that Mama never helped me or believed me it seemed like she swept it under the rug. I always felt like my Mama thought I was lying. Once I got older, I learned that Mr. Jones was molesting me. It made me feel some type of way I felt manipulated like how could someone do that to a child? But hell, James did it to me and I was adult. Men like that just feel like they can do whatever to whomever just like Hakeem felt like he could beat me and verbally abuse me. In life people will abuse you in various ways if you let them. After Hakeem went full force on why we should name the baby A'Deena and not Lisa I was okay with it. He so easily manipulated me and made me do as he wanted. No matter if he hit me, talked down on me I was his baby mama the woman he loved so I knew I had a special place in his heart. And not only that but I knew that this was the best situation for the both of us, I loved him, and he loved me nothing could change that or make me think differently. I had to prove that one day on a lunch date with Chiquita. I was still having morning sickness and I was seven months pregnant, but I wanted to get out the house. I called Chiquita and of course she was down to go. Chiquita knew about the beatings, yet she pretended she didn't. She was always bragging about what a perfect couple we were. At this moment I didn't want to think about the abuse the truth was he had not hit me in months, so I felt like he was really trying. We met at Olive Garden so that I could eat soup. For some reason my phone was messing up all that day and my internet was not working. But I was okay with that, but I did like to look at YouTube videos. I made it to the restaurant first and surprisingly I felt good that day. Chiquita walked in looking as beautiful as ever with her full figure. I stood up and she gave me a kiss on the cheek. "Hey baby doll how you doing?" She asked and sipped some of her lemon water. I knew she loved lemon water, so I ordered her a glass. "I am doing good sis. Never felt better." I meant it too everything was going good with Hakeem we were in love and we were having our second child. Chiquita was a loner she focused solely on her career as a fashion designer. She was big, beautiful, and bold. "Well guess what I have a new man in my life." Chiquita said and I almost lost my lunch. I had never known she was really into men I kind of assumed she was a lesbian like Vanessa. "Don't look at me like that." "I'm just shocked." I said being honest. "I know I am so private with my love life," we both laughed at that. She told me all about Lawrence her great man and I can say I was truly happy for her and I really did feel like she had found someone special. After we talked about her fairy tale lifestyle, she got on me. One thing about people when they think that their life is going in the right path, they are quick to judge you. She had never spoken about me and her brother situation before. Anytime I called her with problems she would say everything would get better and leave it like that. But today since she had found the man of her dreams, she felt like my situation was not up to her standards. "So, when are you and my brother getting married?" I looked at her and shrugged my shoulders. "Have y'all even discussed the possibility?" I shook my head no. "Sweetie you have to learn to be more aggressive with that man he will just make you his baby mama and that's it and after years of bullshit he will get married to someone else and leave you with nothing." Although at the time I felt she was hating, and I didn't want to hear it now I knew she was absolutely right. After Hakeem's death the kids and I were living in a hotel with nothing to our name. Mya was paying the hotel bill for me and I appreciated it. So yes, somethings that people tell us we should listen to it and also learn from it. They may be saying it in what we feel is in a bad way and with bad intentions, but it also may have truth in it. We only know our truth from our point of view but on the outside looking in others see a whole different life. Chiquita's advice was a woman to woman advice that my mother should have taught me. Never depend solely on a man and never put all your eggs in one basket. Hakeem Niya had been gone for a minute and I was mad as fuck where the fuck was she? I left the house that was getting rehabilitated and rushed through the city. I drove to Malcolm's daycare to see if she was there and she wasn't. I drove to her gym to see if she was there and nope, she wasn't. I checked the GPS tracker again and I still did not have a signal. FUCK!

I had my nigga Charles who was tech savvy put a tracker in her phone when she first moved in. I had been driving through the city damn near running lights looking for her. I was surprised my ass didn't get a ticket. I started towards the house I didn't want to call her I just wanted to know where the fuck she was. Fuck it I called Charles. Damn this nigga phone was ringing for a long ass time. "Pick up stupid ass nigga!" I yelled into the phone and he picked up. "What up nigga?" "What up Keem what's good?" My chest started to feel tight and I could hardly breathe. I sped up the car. Shit! This punk ass asthma, "Bro, you know that…" "Aye nigga you alright?" Charles was asking but I could barely breath. Shit! I needed to make it home. I hung up the phone and I was happy as hell that I was at the end of my block. I flew to my house. I jumped out the car and tried to get to the house in a hurry. My damn chest was tightening up. I really needed to keep my asthma pump in the car. Fuck! God please don't let a nigga fall out. Somehow, I made it to the room, and I turned on my damn breathing machine on quickly. That shit was a breath of fresh air. I squeezed some more medicine into the tube and breathed deeply. I could feel the air getting in my lungs and I felt way fucking better. I grabbed my phone and texted Charles as I received my treatment. He replied back and said that she must have her internet data off. I heard Niya walking in the front door. I was feeling better, but I just wanted her to feel sorry for me, so I kept the mask on my face. She walked in the room and looked irritat ed. Bitch what the fuck you irritated for and I damn near died trying to search the city for your stupid ass. I felt like slapping the bitch, but she was pregnant with my daughter. I was so fucking happy that she was having me a girl that I had stopped beating her ass. Wasn't nothing like Daddy's little girl well that is what my Daddy made it seem like because my sister Nessa was his everything. He treated me, his son like shit. That started pissing me off just thinking about his ass. I snatched the mask off my face and jumped up off the bed. "Where the fuck you been?" I growled. She moved back she knew I was seeing red and that I wanted to beat her ass. "I went to Olive Garden with Quita." She replied her look softened and she hugged me. Damn she smelled so good and she felt so soft. My baby was having me a girl. I needed to calm the fuck down she was my everything. I released her and calmly asked. "Where is your phone and why your internet not working?" "How you know my internet not working?" She looked puzzled. Pulling h er phone out of her purse she handed it to me. I went to her settings and turned the data back on. She looked at me funny. "How you knew my internet was messed up?" I didn't even answer her question I never wanted her to know that I was tracking her but fuck it "Next time make sure your settings are set correctly."

Chapter Thirteen
ANIYA

Hakeem had seriously lost his muthafucking mind. A damn tracker on my phone, what the fuck! I could have just bought another phone but then what the nigga would have just put another damn tracker on my phone. I was pissed but also felt good that he loved me so much that he wanted to track me. Yes, I was a ball of confusion but after I had Deena things started to get clear to me. In the crystal ball it showed that Hakeem was crazy, I mean really fucking crazy! After I had Deena you would have thought that things would have been better, but it only got worse. The next three years of my life was pure hell. Hakeem was like a man I had never known. He had beaten me for years but now he had taken things to a whole another ball game. He would slap me, choke me, or even punch me but now his beatings were becoming brutal. He got back to beating me when Deena was about a week old. I had normal labor just like Malcolm. But Deena was a crier she wasn't a sweet quiet baby like Malcolm oh no she liked to cry. Hakeem felt like I was doing something to his baby because she would be crying and after a week of hearing that he showed me how much he had not changed for the better. It was midnight and I had gone into the kid's room because Deena would not stop crying. I think she had colic, but I was not for sure. I had tried everything rocking, feeding, laying her on her stomach but she was wailing, and I was exhausted. I guess Hakeem had been up because he could not sleep because of the crying that girl had a set of lungs on her. He came in the room and told me that he was trying to get some rest and I needed to get her quiet. And I tried but thirty minutes later and all that yelling, and he came back to see why the baby was still crying. "What the fuck Niya do you not know what you are doing?" He asked and grabbed Deena she stopped crying. "I am trying but she is a fucking cry baby I can't deal with that." I got up and walked to our room I was exhausted, and I really didn't want to deal with her or him. Shit since she loved his ass so much, he could deal with her, I lied on the bed and it felt so good that I must have dozed off because I was awaken to an excruciating pain to my stomach. I jumped up in pain. "OOOOOOOOUUUUCCH!!!" There was Hakeem standing over me. He looked like the devil in the flesh. "You trifling ass bitch you just had this baby and now your lazy ass act like I'm supposed to take care of her." He grabbed my short hair and dragged me off the bed his strong ass hands had a tight grip on my hair. My hair was only about three inches long, so the nigga was pulling from the root. I was screaming for him to get off me. "Hakeem! Stop please! Stop!" "Bitch shut the fuck up before you wake these kids up!" He hollered as he dragged me out of the house into the cold. That nigga literally dragged me from my hair down all those damn fifteen steps. My body was being dragged through the hallway of a damn apartment complex and no one came to help. I was in tears. He threw my ass out the front door of the building. When I felt that damn cold wind hit my ass I tried to get up and he punched me in my chest, and it knocked my breath out of my body. I gasped for air. "Naw bitch since you don't wanna take care of these kids you lay your ass outside." He said and slammed the door. It happened to be a cool night and I was thankful I had on some pants and a long sleeve shirt. As my bare feet walked across the grass to my car, I was happy that I always kept my doors unlocked. We lived in a pretty decent neighborhood, so I wasn't worried about someone stealing my car. My concern was that one day I would need to get away from Hakeem and I wouldn't have my car keys. My spare car key was in the visor, but I didn't want to alarm him. If I ever did leave, I was making sure my kids were with me. As I reclined my seat back, I laid my head on the headrest of my passenger seat and fell asleep in tears I was so tired I couldn't even think. Hakeem knocked on my window the next morning and woke me up. I didn't say anything I just got out the car and went back into the house. My chest still hurt, and I knew there was a bruise there. My stomach was hurting so bad that I felt like I was in labor all over again. But I didn't say anything all the pain that was shooting through my body was nothing compared to pain that I felt on the inside I was hurt. I didn't even cry as I let the water run across my bruised body, I just washed my ass and got out and got Deena. I was happy Malcolm still went to daycare because I needed as much sleep as possible during the day. When she slept, I slept. I didn't have any money, so I had to tell Hakeem to buy her some medicine to help with the colic. When I called him, he acted normal like he had not just beat my ass. He did as I asked and bought her some medicine. Hakeem Muthafuckas probably say that I ain't shit because I be having to put Niya in check but shit this the only way I know. Don't get me wrong I stayed taking my bitch out to dinner, movies, all that good shit. We always had the time of our lives when we were together, but it was just sometimes I had to check the bitch. I had tried to talk to Quita about why I was so abusive and what I could do to stop it. But all she would say is "nigga you a man and she be fucking up you need to check that bitch." What kind of shit is that? I bet if it was her, she would be quick to call me to whoop a nigga ass and I would be there. I had no structure and I was grateful that Niya had never called the police on me. She was a real bitch she would just rest up and get back to it like nothing happened. But I think the worst I had ever done was when I broke her jaw after she had Deena. That was some foul shit, but I was pissed at her because I had lost a damn cleaning contract that day at work and shit her ass was talking shit. I told her to make some food and she just had to get smart. "I am tired can't you just order something" she said. She didn't even have an attitude I was just pissed and because I was pissed, I punched her ass so hard that I broke her jaw. This was a bruise that could not easily be hidden. I had to take her to hospital, and they called the police. When the police came, she said that she ran into a tree. She bought home some damn pamphlets on domestic violence and I made sure to tear that shit up. As I lay next to Niya in the bed that night her fragrance takes over my nostrils. She is so beautiful, and I love her so much. I know she hates me I know she can't stand me, but I try, I really try. Damn I was wondering how she was feeling. "Niya baby you love me?" "Yeah" she answered the shit sounded unbelievable. She turned and faced me. "I know I be fucking up ma. What is your best thought of me?" I asked as I looked into her hazel brown eyes. She looked up at me and smiled and I could see love in her eyes. "You remember when you took me to the Sybaris?" The look on her face was priceless. It was Valentine's Day weekend before Deena was born and I went all out for my baby. I had called to make sure Quita was still getting Malcolm so we could enjoy ourselves. Niya didn't know what I had planned but she knew I had something going on for us. I didn't even go to work and when she walked in the house, I made sure she saw the dozen red roses on the kitchen table. It had a note attached to it "I am coming to get you in an hour be ready" that was all it read. I had to go catch up with this young bitch

Malena I had been fucking on, so I knew she had to get ready anyways. Malena was this little hoe that I fucked on from time to time, but she had a man some little weak ass nigga named Chance. I had seen the nigga a couple of times when we had close calls, but he didn't know I was fucking her. Malena was okay a Puerto Rican chick with a big ass and titties, but nobody was finer than bitch and that was for sure. When I got back to the house Niya was looking good as fuck. She had on a white sweater dress with the big neck and some long red thigh high boots. She was still fixing her make-up when I came in the door. I came behind her and kissed her neck. That damn Beyonce perfume "Heat" was definitely turning me the fuck on. "Damn baby you so sexy." She twirled around and kissed me. "You sexy too baby." She said I knew I was. I had just got a fresh lining and my curls were looking good. I had on some black slacks with a white button up shirt. She turned back around and put my arms around her waist. That big ass was right on my dick. "We look so good together," she said, and I had to agree. Her eyes sparkled with love. "Come on baby," I told her as we made our way out the door. "Damn baby I don't know if we gone make it to the room." She giggled as we left out the house. It was a long drive to the Sybaris but when we got to Mequon it was worth the it. The mirrors, the bed, the water, a nigga was ready to fuck. But I wanted to take it nice and slow. Niya was feeling good and I could tell as she sipped on her Champagne. She was giggling and laughing, and I knew that she still had love for a nigga. I know I mistreated her at times but that was how it was shit I couldn't do anything about that. That I night I made it up to her. I fucked her for the bullshit I had put her through and the past, present, and the near future. As I made love to her and looked in her beautiful face, I knew that she was my everything and that she would never leave me. I loved the way she was moaning my name "Hakeem" yup this was my bitch forever. I smiled to myself when she told me that was her favorite time yes that was a good time and I just wanted her to remember that every time I hurt her. I wanted her to feel that special way every time she felt like she was going to give up on me. I loved her and although I hurt her, I knew that she loved me. It was just my past had fucked me up, I didn't know how to deal with it.

Chapter Fourteen
ANIYA

fter two buses of crazy people we finally made it to the insurance company. I was excited I am not going to lie. I didn't have a dime to my name thanks to my stupidity of giving everything to Hakeem. And after Hakeem died Chiquita who swore up and down that I killed her brother came and took over my apartment. It was a week after his funeral, and I was making the kids lunch. Hell, I had moved on from the whole situation he was my kid's father, but he was a nasty man and I was relieved he was gone. No lie I was in shock, but he was beating me, so I was happy that I no longer had to endure that. I heard the key turn in the lock and the door opened and in walked Chiquita. She and I had had a great relationship but under the circumstances on how her brother died she felt as if I wasn't shit and it could have been prevented. Yes, it could have if he had not been whooping my ass. "Yall still here?" She asked walking in. "Excuse me." I said looking at her like she had lost her mind. "Since this was my brother's place, I plan on keeping it, but you bitch you have to go!" She yelled. In walked Lawrence her man. He was fine too. He was a dark-skinned man with a low haircut, and 6'2. "Quita baby I told you don't come over here starting mess now talk to this lady like you got some sense." She rolled her eyes. "Look you can stay here until next week but you gotta go the kids can come with me." "You got me fucked up if you think you are getting my kids." I said and continued to feed my kids. I would be out of there next week, but I didn't know where I was going to go or how I would survive. Thanks to Mya for putting us up in a hotel. We had remained friends over the years and she knew very little about the abuse that Hakeem was putting me through. She was also the kids godmother, so she always looked out for me. She didn't understand why I didn't have any money and I didn't know how to explain it to her. Yes, Hakeem had money in the bank but I wasn't his wife so I couldn't go and take the money out. So here we were now standing outside of the insurance building. I had asked Mya for so much I wouldn't dare ask her to take me anywhere. I was in a state of depression and all I had was myself at this moment, well and of course my kids. I walked into the lobby of the insurance company and a familiarity went through my body. Just like when Mama died, I thought, and she had the same insurance also. All that money gone to waste, I walked up to the receptionist and gave her my name. "Hello, my name is Aniya Turner you all called me earlier." I said, damn I had forgot to get a name I was too excited when they called. "Oh yes Mr. Williams is expecting you." She said and called him on the phone. I had seen Mr. Williams when I had got my insurance money for Mama, damn he was still alive. He was an old, short, white man. He had white hair, I think he was damn near 90 or he aged hard. Mr. Williams came out and got me in the kids and we went to his office. "Ms. Turner back again and so soon." He was sympathetic. I just shook my head with tears in my eyes. "Well, let's get down to it. Mr. Harris your significant other named you as sole beneficiary for his half a million-dollar policy as you may know." I looked confused because I didn't know. "So, do you want this money deposited into you all bank account?" "I don't have a bank account." I said. Sounding and looking sad. Shit I didn't I had closed my bank account and allowed Hakeem to run everything how stupid of me. "Well I talked with Mr. Harris's lawyer and she said that you guys had a joint bank account." I didn't know anything about it, but I was sure going to give this lawyer a call. "Well do you have his lawyer's phone number?" I didn't know Hakeem had a lawyer. "Sure Ms. Turner her name is Susan Walker." He gave me her number. "So, did you want it deposited into the bank account?" He asked again. "No, I will take a check." I said. I gathered up my kids and we were off to find some answers. I wanted to know about this joint bank account, and how did they know to call me. I remember when Mama died, I had to call the insurance company and get a death certificate and everything. Half a million dollars that was a lot of money damn Hakeem thank you! It took us two hours to get back to the hotel, but we did. The kids was exhausted and so was I. We ordered room service and watched television. My mind was everywhere though. Five hundred thousand dollars! Damn just when I was thinking about going to a shelter God was blessing me. I cried not for Hakeem, not for my kids, but for me. It felt good to purge my soul. I had held in all the pain for so many years. Hell, after so much abuse I didn't even cry. I remember when Deena was about 5 months and Hakeem and I had gotten into it. He was mad because I made dinner to early and his food was not hot enough. "Damn Hakeem I will just warm it up in the microwave," I said with an attitude. I needed to study, and all this jerk could think about was some damn food. I had gone back to school when Deena was 3 months old. He didn't say anything he just got up and warmed his own plate up. I stormed off and went to the kid's room to study. Malcolm was watching cartoons in his toddler bed and Deena was napping. I guess after he ate, he called me in our room. I didn't want to go but I got up anyways. I walked into the bedroom and he told me to come here. I had on some shorts that day with a wife beater. He grabbed my arm and before I knew it, I was bent over his knee and he was whipping my ass. The belt hit my ass and at this time I was so numb to the beatings that I didn't even cry or scream. My mind just drifted away I had learned to block out the pain. He had done so many cruel things to me that nothing actually hurt me my wounds were a permanent ache on my heart. He was pissed that I didn't cry either. I got up and I looked at him he said, "oh that shit didn't hurt huh, so you tough as nails huh?" I didn't say anything I just stood there and that pissed him off. He hauled off and punched me in the eye. I grabbed my eye, but I still didn't cry. "You ain't got to cry bitch I can see the pain from that black eye I gave you." He said and started laughing. I couldn't even study my eye was swollen shut. I didn't cry though I laid in the big bed with Deena and thought about how long I would be out of school this time because of my eye. Yes, Hakeem the father of my children he beat me yes, he abused me, and yes, I loved me. He was all I knew, and he was all I had. He wanted it that way too he saw a little vulnerable woman and he took advantage. I had let him in too fast and told him too much within a couple of hours. No wonder he didn't have a woman as fine as he was, he was evil he was the devil. I often wondered did he ever feel remorse for what he did. In the beginning it seemed like he cared but that was really only to make me stay because after years and years of abuse he never stopped. He only got worse with time. It was like he was trying to kill me or break me. I never knew why he was so angry I had been nothing but good to the man. Yes, I talked back and spoke up for myself because I was a grown woman not just that I am a person and we all need to express ourselves. He made me not want to express myself, he made me feel small and weak. And although I knew it was going to be a struggle raising two kids on my own, I was happy he was gone. I really was.

Chapter Fifteen

ANIYA

The next day I felt a whole lot better. The kids were still sleep so I jumped in the shower. Over the last couple of weeks, I had lost weight from all the stress. When I got out the shower, I ordered the kids some breakfast. I couldn't eat I had too much on my mind. I had to call the lawyer's office today. I dialed her number. Her receptionist picked up and transferred the call. "Finally, girl I have been trying to get in touch with you for weeks." She said as soon as the call had transferred. "Hi, I been in a slump." I said and that was the truth. "Yes, I know, I can't even imagine losing my husband we have been together for fifteen years now." There was silence I didn't know what to say Hakeem wasn't my husband and to be honest

I was happy he was gone. "Well, Chiquita came calling me when the tragic events happened and that's how I found out. She is such a bossy bitch." She said and I laughed. "She swears that Hakeem had a policy with her name as the beneficiary which is bullshit. I know that she paid for the funeral and everything, so I don't know if you want to repay her. Since I am her attorney too, I would say fuck her, because she did it nobody asked her too." The lady was right I bet when Chiquita found out I had all the money she would try to sue me or some bullshit like that. "I have all the bank information he had the kids trust funds of a hundred thousand dollars each. I know he was very adamant on Cedes not getting anything, but he set up the kids a twenty-thousand-dollar trust fund. You don't have to continue to pay into those if you don't want too." "Cedes? What does she have to do with any of this?" I asked. Cedes was Vanessa's girlfriend so why and the hell was Hakeem putting a trust fund aside for her three boys. "Well she doesn't have anything to do with this their kids do he wanted to make sure everyone was straight." She was talking but after that I heard nothing. So, you mean to tell me that Cedes was Hakeem's baby mama too? Well how in the hell did I not know this shit? Here I was taking this man shit for seven years and he had other kids. The things you don't realize that's right under your nose. So, he had been lying to me the entire time. "So, are you coming to sign the papers today?" She asked. "Ummm sure I will see if my friend can bring me." We hung up the phone and my head was spinning I needed to lie down, but the kids were woke now. To think all this time that son of a bitch was lying to me. He had other kids, three other kids to be exact and I knew who they were. All the times I had seen Cedes and her three boys and that bitch just sat in my face smiling like everything was okay, those fake bitches. I never really had a relationship with Vanessa anyways she just said hi and bye and kept mostly to herself but that bitch Chiquita she knew that shit. I called Mya and asked her to take me to the attorney's office. I didn't know what I was signing but hell I was going. I needed to get past this me and my kids. Fuck Hakeem we deserved everything that was coming to us and he deserved that grave that he was in. She came in an hour and I was so happy for that. Mya was a true friend and one day I would be a true friend to her and tell her all the things she needed to know about me, yeah one day. Mrs. Walker's office was beautiful you could tell she had money. Her receptionist was a young white girl with long blonde hair. I walked up to her desk. "Hi I am her to see Mrs. Walker my name is Aniya Turner."

She called her on the phone. Mrs. Walker didn't have me wait at all she came out right away. She was a slim older white lady who was maybe in her early forties. She also had blonde hair but hers was short and curly. She gave me a hug and her scent was marvelous, "I am so sorry honey." She said. Her embrace made me cry not because of Hakeem but because I had never been embraced like this before. She had a mother's touch and that was something I needed at this very moment not just at this moment, but this was something I was missing all of my life. That hug did something for me and I could barely stand up she held on though. And I could tell she was a very sincere woman. No one had showed me this type of love except for Mya. Mya was there for me when Hakeem died. She held my hand at the church. Chiquita told me I couldn't come to his homecoming, so I went early me and the kids to pay our respects. She made sure Hakeem was looking nice too. He had on an all-black suit which was his favorite color. He looked a bit darker than his light skin but other than that he looked like Hakeem. It was hard for the kids. Malcolm knew what was going on and he cried. But Deena she really didn't understand she just kept saying, "Daddy sleep for a long time, Mama wake him up." At that moment I did cry I cried like a baby. Mya was there to be a shoulder to lean on, but I was at my wits end. I didn't know what to do at the time I mean I really did love the man. No, he wasn't perfect, but he belonged to me. And although he took every bit and piece of me and tried to ruin me, I still couldn't help but love him. I knew that deep down Hakeem really loved me. But he just didn't know how to show it. And that saddened me a lot of times after he would beat me, I would clean myself up and go lay and cuddle next to him. He would let me too he would never really be mad after the beatings he would always want to feel my touch. And when I didn't get in the bed with him, he didn't make a fuss he let me have my space. One particular night he had beat me up. He was mad because he wanted to watch the game and I was talking too loud to the kids. He wanted me to shut up, so he dragged me through the house by my hair. I got in the bed with him and I got on top of him and just cuddled. He kissed me on my forehead and said, "I love you so much Niya." I said, "I love you too baby." Moments like that were few but those were the moments that I loved about him. I loved those sexy eyes that seemed to speak to me even when he said no words. I loved those big juicy lips the ones that when he kissed you it made your heart melt. I loved that baby soft skin when I would rub lotion over his body it made his skin feel soft as butter.

I loved that voice with so much authority yet so much passion. Yes, those were the things I loved most and missed most about my man, but he was gone now. And I was alone. I thought that I would at least have Chiquita but nope I didn't have her either. Chiquita had been like a big sister to me but when Hakeem died, she showed who her loyalty belonged to, her brother. Shit all these years she had showed me who her loyalty belonged to I just never paid attention. From day one she knew Hakeem was beating on me and she always encouraged me to stick it through. But the truth is if Lawrence was beating her ass Hakeem would have come over there and beat him so bad and Chiquita would not had stayed. But when it's not them they think it is okay. She would say shit like "that's a man for you", "he loves you he just doesn't know how to show it honey," and her favorite when we had the kids "oh girl you gone take his kids away from him yall are all he have." Yes, one thing is for sure I didn't know it then but now I definitely knew it now her loyalty was with her brother. After I finally got myself together Mrs. Walker took me in her office, and I cleaned myself up. I sat in the big leather chair on the opposite of her cherry wood rectangular desk. "So, these are the papers." She had a couple of papers for me to sign. "Like I told you before all the money in the bank account is yours, and the businesses are all yours you have to get that all together. Hakeem said you was going to school for business so I know that will be a walk in a park for you." Yup he bragged on me in public but beat me at home. The definition of a true deceiver, Hakeem was. It was true I had completed my Bachelor's Degree in Business. I was proud of myself and Hakeem was also proud of me. My graduation you should have seen him sitting in the audience with our beautiful children. That was just a couple of months ago and now this tragedy. Hakeem was so proud of me he even rented me out some office space. He said, "now I don't know what kind of business you ready to start with two little ones but just know that I am behind you one hundred percent." That made me happy those little small gestures were the things that made me stay. Those little gestures which made me happy also confused me. He would be so supportive one day yet ready to whoop my ass over one small mistake. His loyalty and love was a mystery to me. How could he love me so deep yet beat me so horrific? I signed the papers and thanked Mrs. Walker for all her help. I got my papers together and told Mya to take me to the bank. I was so excited I didn't know what to do. I had money. Now I could go get my car out the shop. I had wrecked my car the day that Hakeem had died. So, with no money I couldn't get it out the shop but with a five hundred-thousand-dollar check burning a hole in my purse I was ready to get my baby back. I asked Mya to wait in the car with the kid's just like at the attorney's office. She agreed and didn't ask any questions. I walked in the bank and felt like a new woman. I asked for the bank manager and was met by a white guy. His name was Gary Bird and he was awesome. I made sure I brought Hakeem's death certificate so that he could be taken off of the account. I showed him the papers from the lawyer, and I was set. I deposited my half a million-dollar check in the account which brought my account to one million one thousand two hundred forty-eight dollars and twenty-nine cents. I kept the receipt to remind myself that I had money. The check had to clear in seven days, but the other money was up for grabs. I told Mya to drop me off at the car shop. I picked up my car and it was beautiful just like before. That candy red apple Porsche was my baby. I still had the kid's car seat in the back. I rode back to the hotel. I decided to let the kids play in the swimming pool while I thought of a master plan. Oh yes, I had money and all the things that I dreamed was going to come true.

Chapter Sixteen

NIYA

I decided to stay in the hotel until I had finished conducting my business. Mya's family owned the hotel where I was staying. I didn't have to pay or anything she was footing the bill; if there was one. Two long weeks of sitting in that hotel broke and crying, now I was a rich woman and I would not be a fool. I had to make smart choices so that I could live comfortably after all the shit I went through with Hakeem a bitch deserved it. First thing first was to see about all his businesses. He had a cleaning company, a carpentry business, and he rebuilt homes. I would have loved to keep all the companies but after careful consideration I decided to focus on the cleaning company. I went to talk to some of his employees.

I let them know if they could put, they money together and buy me out then I would sell to them. I decided to wait everything out for a week to see what was what before I decided to buy a house. We would live in the hotel until then. That night as we said our prayers and I tucked my kids in the bed I felt grateful that the struggle was finally over. I was going to be able to take care of them and most importantly we were safe. My phone rung just as I was nodding off. I saw that it was Chiquita, I didn't want to talk to her, but I answered anyways. "Hello," I said. "So, Mrs. Walker told me that you got all of Hakeem's money," she said spitefully. "Well if you think that I am going to take this and let it ride then bitch you got another thing coming." "Chiquita you must be crazy!" I screamed she was making me mad now. All the shit I put up with her brother I was not about to put up with her shit in his death I needed peace, I deserved peace. "Yes, bitch that's right I am crazy! You think that my brother was whooping your ass bitch I am going to give you an ass whooping you wouldn't believe." The audacity of this bitch to even bring up some hurtful shit, she had hurt my feelings. With all the pain that Hakeem had put me through I could take it and I had learned how to dish it out. "You know what you funky bitch fuck you," I said in a quiet tone. I was mad but

I was not going to make my kids up arguing with this hoe. "You think I was taking ass whooping from a man and you gone whoop my ass? You got another thing coming you stupid hoe one thing I learned is how to take a hit and how to give it out. You can come get this ass whooping if you want it." I gave Chiquita my room number and jumped out of the bed. I put my shoes on my blood was boiling. I sat in the chair and waited for that bitch to come knock on my door. I had bail money, so I wasn't worried about the police being called. One thing about me I was not a punk I had taken many ass whooping from my man; but I would be damned if a woman would punk me out. Hakeem had taught me not to take shit from nobody only him. I recall we were in the parking lot at the grocery store and some lady took the spot that Hakeem wanted. Hakeem was pissed. He yelled out the window of his car, "now you know I was about to get in that spot." She rolled her green contacts and smacked her lips and said "fuck you." I couldn't believe that bitch had talked to my man like that. Before I knew it, I had jumped out the car and was on her ass. I punched her so hard she stumbled backwards. One of her home girls must have thought that they could jump in, but I saw her coming and punched her skinny ass right to the ground and she was smart enough to stay there. I pounced back on the main chick and tore into her ass. I was punching her so quickly and fast you would have thought I was on of Muhammed Ali's daughter. My kids got to crying and Hakeem grabbed me, and we drove off. We laughed our ass off the whole way to another store. I waited and waited, and Chiquita never showed up bet not had because I was ready to whoop her ass. Not for just talking shit to me but for sitting in my face lying pretending to be my friend when all along she knew the truth. She was low down and dirty and she had the nerve to kick me out of my house. The house I had stayed in the house that I paid rent in. She had me all the way fucked up she knew not to come because she knew I would have beat her ass. When you are in an abusive relationship you change as a person and I knew that I had changed as a person. I became tougher. Nobody could sit and talk to me anyway or I would go off not because I was afraid but because I was taking so much disrespect at home that I felt everyone else needed to respect me. Nope I couldn't get respect from my man, so I wanted others to respect me, so I lashed out. The only people I didn't lash out on were Mya, Chiquita, and Hakeem. It was time for the kids to get into some type of summer day camp or something. I needed the days for me to sort everything out. I signed them up for day camp at the YMCA and paid my fees upfront. I needed to get my business together and I could not do that carrying two children around. They seemed okay though because they both had been going to daycare since they were infants. Malcolm seemed to be taking the death of his father well. I told them Daddy was in heaven looking down on us. Malcolm asked me, "Mama did Jesus take Dad away from us because he hurt you?" and I didn't know how to answer. It was sad that my children had witnessed the abuse between me and their father and although he was wrong so was I. I was wrong for allowing my children to see me get beat on. No one should go through abuse but the truth is so many women do, and we sit and let our children see it. No parent is perfect, but somethings just will never sit right with me and that is one thing that will never sit right with me. I allowed my children to see me get beat. Deena she wasn't really sure what was going on she thought that her Daddy was taking a nap. She loved her Daddy and I felt she loved him more than she loved me, but she had to learn to live without him. She asked about him every day because she was so used to him hugging her and sitting in front of the television with her watching cartoons. He never really paid too much attention to Malcolm. After a week I went to the carpentry business and the fellas had gathered up their money and bought me out. The carpentry business only made two hundred thousand a year, so I accepted one hundred and fifty thousand and signed over the papers. The men who worked for the company that built the houses didn't have enough money to buy me out so I met a young man that could. He loved the idea that Hakeem and I came up with. We had so much money we went around to foreclosed homes and bought them at the auction and fixed them up and rented them out. We had a very good crew and I really did not want to fire them so that is why I was looking for someone to take over and keep the crew. Bruce was a young white man with brown hair and green eyes. He was gorgeous to say the least. He bought me out for half a million dollars. We had at least two dozen properties that were already built and rented out and that grossed in at a million dollars a year, so I took the short end of the stick. I really did want to keep that business I loved it. I would always go with Hakeem when a house was finished and look it over. The work them men did was marvelous. I knew that I would not be able to keep us in business because I had other things to do and being a single mother of two was not going to be easy. Although Bruce was willing to buy me out, he felt like I was losing money so he said that he would leave me as a partner and that I could get ten percent of whatever he made. I never thought about just being a partner and letting someone else run it. Bruce was a smart man he had many degrees and was very educated. When I went to his office his accomplishments were hanging on his wall and it made my pussy moist. I knew that he was the perfect person to do business with or was it those green eyes? I was attracted to Bruce and the feeling was mutual. I walked in his office that hot summer day with a red skirt that was a good length but above the knees, I had on strapless white shirt because it was so hot. I still had my short haircut. I sat at his desk and his eyes went straight to my thighs. I had slimmed down over the last couple of weeks the wonders that stress could do to your body. I was fitting in a size fourteen and I loved it. My stomach had always been flat, and my titties were still little. "Hello Bruce, you needed me to come down and sign some papers?" I asked. "Yes, Mrs. Walker sent them back to me." He looked me up and down. I had sent the documents to Mrs. Walker to make sure everything was straight, and she said it was okay. She told me to let her send them back to him to reassure him that I was smart and did have legal advice. She told me the truth. She said these white educated men will think black women like yourself is stupid I know I'm white and I hear their conversations. I know she had the best interest for me that is why I kept her as my lawyer. Bruce, I felt that he was different, or maybe it was because he was attractive. "Yes, you know I am not really good at this, so I had to make sure everything was legit." Why did I say that stupid shit now he thinks I don't know anything. He didn't say anything else he just handed me the papers as he handed them to me our hands touched, and my nipples got erect. I looked into his green eyes, damn I hadn't had sex in a long time. Bruce always made me feel comfortable and when I looked in those green eyes, I saw peace. I had been talking and texting him for a week about business and although it was about business, he always wanted to get personal. Like the first time we met, we met at a restaurant and we had lunch. I must have had something on my face because he wiped it off, that was too intimate to me that was something my man would do. That was something my man should do but Hakeem never did anything like that if I had something on my lip in public Hakeem would look at me in disgust and say, "ugh bitch wipe your mouth." Those were the harsh words I was used to not the kind gesture that Bruce had showed me. After I signed the papers, I was ready to go. The central air was on full blast, but I was hot. "So beautiful my first task is I want to find you a house for you and your kids." I had told him about us living in the hotel. I didn't think about that idea but since we were in business together then that would be great. That way I could get my house built the way that I wanted, and I knew the work would be great. "You know what that is a great idea. But I want a lot of things and I need it done right." I laughed I was being so bossy. "Of course, beautiful tell me what you want." I told him everything I wanted a pool with a big back yard with a play area for the kids, a master bedroom with a master bathroom. I needed a room for Deena and a room for Malcolm. I needed an office and I also needed an indoor playroom for the kids. I wanted an open kitchen with a dining room. I needed a big living room and a finished basement. He soaked it up and told me he could deliver I hope he could.

Chapter Seventeen
ANIYA

As the wind hit my face, I sobered up a bit. Was that really the wind or did Hakeem just smack me across my face? It scared me I felt like maybe it was my drink getting to me, but I wasn't ready to leave with Bruce. Yes, I was lonely, and it was true I was horny but all the liquor in the world could not prepare me right now to be intimate with someone. I still felt a weird feeling like Hakeem would see me. "I'm sorry Bruce I can't do this." I said and ran to my car. My heart was racing, and I needed to get myself together. I made it to the car and dropped my keys before I could click the lock. I went to pick up the keys and I felt someone behind me. I thought I was being robbed I grabbed my pepper spray. But before

I could spray it Bruce grabbed my arm. "Hey, hey, babe you are acting crazy!" He said calming me down. "I'm sorry Bruce it's just that… I thought… I have to go." He let my arm go I went down to grab my keys. I knew I was acting like a crazy woman, but I did not care at that very moment I needed to get in a safe place. "Calm down I understand. I just want you to get home safe and you need to calm down. You ran from me like I was going to hurt you." I looked at him, "you might," I said and got in my car and drove away. The entire ride home my mind was going back and forth. After we closed the deals on the business Bruce had asked me out. We went for drinks and dinner he was a perfect gentlemen. I liked Bruce and as we kissed in the restaurant, I felt like I wanted to take things to the bedroom; I was wrong. As I pulled into my parking spot, I looked in the mirror at my reflection the tears highlighted my cheeks, I was not over Hakeem. The next few days I stayed to myself. I conducted business but I felt like a fool. I thought I was ready to move but I wasn't. Bruce had been calling to check on me, but I was so embarrassed that I ignored all of his calls I bet he thought I was a crazy woman. I know he thought it because I thought that way about myself. Here I was a twenty-nine-year old woman running down the damn street from a man I had known for months. We were business partners how much harm could he do me? The cleaning business was in high demand. Ever since I took over with all my marketing and advertising, we were getting more business which was perfect for me, but I still had not found a Nanny/ Personal Assistant yet. Right now, that was my main goal to find someone to help me organize my life. I was used to being with my kids all the time and now I barely had time for them. I was always in my office or out during the day. It was exhausting and I felt that I was neglecting them. I put an ad on craigslist and ran into so many crazy people I was ready to give up. There was a man who I called who thought I needed a sex slave, and then there was a woman who got passed the phone interview process she seemed like the perfect candidate but as soon as I met her in person, I knew she was all wrong. I told her to meet me at Applebee's of course lunch was on me. She came in with purple hair, purple lipstick, and all types of piercings. I could not allow her around my children she would scare them. She was saying weird things as we conversed and was blurting things out, I was done. I was ready to give up but then I got a call from a Mercedes Taylor. She was perfect I called her on the phone, and she was polite, and she had experience with kids. She had not worked in years because of certain situations but I could relate. We decided to meet at IHop for lunch. When I made it to the restaurant, I told the hostess to point the person into my direction and I told Mercedes to say she was with Ms. Turner. I was sipping my hot chocolate when I looked up and saw Cedes. She had on a black blazer with a red skirt. Her makeup was flawless, and her hair was in a short cut which really brought out her features. Huh she looked fantastic as usual but when the hostess brought her to my table I was dazed. This was Mercedes Taylor, my perspective employee. It was okay I was professional and plus we didn't have any bad blood, she was just my baby daddy's other baby mama. She sat down and smiled, "I didn't know your name was Aniya. I thought maybe it was Shaniya or something like that. Isn't this a coincidence?" "Yes, it is very surprising." I said still stunned. How is it that I ended up in this situation? I know she knew my name she had set me up or maybe she did need a job. "Okay so I did know it was you, but I do need a job also. I haven't been to work in years." She said and looked sad, "and I am a really good listener and I know I could help with the kids since I do know them." "Yes, you do know them since we have the same baby daddy, so that would make our kids siblings." I was getting hot. The nerve of her to sit in my face and pretend, she looked defeated, yes bitch the jig was up. "Okay Niya yes my sons are Hakeem's kids, but don't get the wrong idea about me. I am not who you may think I am. I am not trying to manipulate you or get in your business I really do want to help. I really do need help as in a job." "Why didn't anyone tell me he had other kids?" I was almost in tears although I was mad at him, I still loved him. I always would he was my baby daddy. "The same reason why we have matching scars inside and out," she pointed to the scar on my lip where it had been busted so many times it was a permanent scar and she had the same scar but hers was in the upper right-hand side. "The same reason why we having matching tattoos" she laughed, "yeah I know you got his name on your lower back." She was right I did. Yes, we probably did have the same scars, but I knew that mine were a little bit deeper than hers. "Niya just like so many years you lived in fear so did I and when I got out I was content." "But you didn't get out aren't you Vanessa's girlfriend?" I was confused. "Yes, I am, and I will love her forever. She was the one who got me out of there. We fell in love and she was the one who got me away from her crazy, abusive brother. And after I left, he met you." The waitress came back and we decided to order. I was hungry and I really did want to get an understanding of their history. "What happened?" I anticipated the story and I really wanted to know. Here I was angry at the woman, but she was just like me a broken woman. Mercedes I was sitting next to the beautiful Aniya. Yes, Aniya Turner was the love of my baby's daddy life. Hakeem Moore was the nigga who took over my world. She was beautiful and he loved her just as much he loved me but for some reason, he loved her a bit more. He took care of her kids a nd allowed them to know who their father was. I met Hakeem when I was fifteen years old and after about three months, I got pregnant with our first son. He was happy at first and we were in love. I had got put out by my mama and at the time Chiquita, Vanessa, and Hakeem all still st ayed together. I think I was his first real girlfriend. So, they all took me in and treated me just like family. Everything was fine after Junior was born. Hakeem was always a hard-working man and always did take care of us. One day I was tired because I was still going to school during the day. Chiquita was watching Junior and I had come home and laid down. I don't know if Chiquita didn't like me or what, but she told Hakeem that I was a lazy bitch and from then on, he started beating me. I knew that bitch Chiquita had something to do with the way he acted. She had a lot of control over her brother and I think that if she wanted him to stop beating me, I think he would have but that bitch loved the pain of another person. I had Jon-Jon a year later and then I had Chris two years later yes, I had three kids at the age of eighteen and I was in an abusive relationship. I didn't know what to do. Years went by and I took it. Vanessa was always quiet she never really said too much. One day Hakeem had beat me up and I was crying, and I went into Vanessa's room. She was happy that I had finally come to her. She was my savior. It got to the point where Vanessa and Hakeem would argue over me and after a year we moved out. At first Vanessa and I were not dating at first, she was my first woman and I was her first woman, but we fell in love. Hakeem would harass me whenever Vanessa would leave me alone, but he never did anything he never hit me again. He never fought Vanessa and after he found out we were dating he left me alone. When I tried to make him take care of his kids he never did. He disowned them and acted like they didn't exist. I sat there and spilled out my entire story to Aniya. I didn't know what she thought. I had sex with Hakeem sometimes after I had left him. I liked Aniya I could see why he loved her, she radiated grace. "So, did he ever have a girlfriend after you or was I the first?" Aniya questioned with her eyes. "Yeah he did but he beat her up and she had her brothers come and they beat his ass so bad he had an asthma attack, but he survived." It was ironic that he had actually died of an asthma attack. That man did not like to admit that he had asthma. The entire time we were together he never really said anything about having asthma. I had experienced the wheezing at night, the near- death experiences where he almost lost his life, but he managed to survive but not this time. I wonder why? We all had our suspicions but looking at Aniya I knew that she was not capable of killing Hakeem. "Well anyways I am sorry that you went through that with Hakeem and I will hire you," she said, and I was truly happy. I needed to get out and experience life. It had been years since I gotten out and worked and I really needed to become independent. We decided that I would start next week. I would handle all the calls after five o'clock and I would watch the kids after school until five. She needed my help some days to help with business ideas. I was happy that she trusted me.

Chapter Eighteen
ANIYA

It had been six months two weeks and forty-five days since Hakeem had died and I felt good. The business was making top dollars I had so much money in my savings that I could travel anywhere. The kids and I had settled into our new home comfortably, Bruce had done everything I asked of him. I was planning a move with my business an expansion. I had finally decided to talk to Bruce about some plans and he said his brother was well known in Atlanta and could make some things happen that delighted me. Ever since that night at the restaurant Bruce had been nothing but a gentlemen, we even went out a couple of times. Nothing serious just a friendship, that was all I could tolerate. Cedes was still my Nanny/ Personal Assistant and the truth is we were a business match made in heaven. I had even given her a percentage of the business just because of all the things that she had been through with Hakeem. I knew that she told me that everything was good with Vanessa, but I felt like things were not so great in their relationship either. One day Cedes walked in my home since she had a key she came right in and came in the office. "Hey girl what's up?" I said not really paying her any attention I was too busy on the computer going over a weak business proposal. "Nothing," she replied, and I could hear the tears in her voice. I looked up. She looked alright her hair was in a curly weave that had brown streaks. She had on a white shirt and some black slacks. But her face looked different. Cedes was a beautiful woman but it looked as if she had makeup on her face more than usual. Now some women need makeup to hide blemishes or scars. Like me I had scars that I needed to hide my once flawless skin was now bruised and I hated it. Women like Cedes with flawless smooth skin did not need make up. Her skin was a beautiful brown that toasted in the summer and she was gorgeous so why would a beautiful person like her need so much makeup on? She was hiding something, I walked up to her she was on the lounge looking in her laptop. I raised her face up. "Cedes what is going on?" "What do you mean?" She asked. I looked in her eyes and I could tell she had been crying. "Cedes is Vanessa hitting you?" I asked. I had never really spoken to Vanessa because she never really spoke to me. She sometimes dropped Cedes off when her car was in the shop but other than that she never really said anything. "No, she would never hit me." She said shaking her head. "Well what is going on?" I was aggressive I did not want to keep asking her. She sat in silence. "Cedes you know I will never judge you; you are like a sister to me so what is going on?" She sighed but I could tell she wanted to talk and that she was, "I've been cheating on Vanessa with a man." She said and I was in shock. "He hit me yesterday when I told him I was pregnant because he is seeing another woman." "What! That is his fuck up! And he hit you? Oh, he has lost his mind!" I was heated it made me feel like I was getting beaten all over again. I remember the hits I remember not feeling like I was even worth living. Sometimes I would wake up and think about killing myself just like my mom had done. I couldn't imagine going through that type of abuse again. Cedes had suffered at the hands of Hakeem so I didn't understand why she would accept it again. "Well, it's my fuck up too. I should have never started messing around with him." She was right it's karma. My mind went to Hakeem's dead body, I wonder what I ever have to face that bitch karma? I shook the thought out of my head. "Yeah you right but we all make mistakes no man should ever hit a woman though. Do I know the guy who is he?" Cedes never went anywhere that I knew of, so it astonished me that she was even having an affair. "Lawrence," she said in a whisper. Oh no not Chiquita's man Lawrence. I started laughing. Oh, how the table's turned. That bitch Chiquita I bet didn't know. I had seen them last week at the mall and she didn't even speak to the kids. I didn't give a fuck she kept calling my phone private talking about I killed her brother. She was crazy on his death certificate it said natural cause of death so that is what it is. She even had the nerve to some detectives come and question me about a month ago. She said it seemed suspicious that he didn't have his inhaler near. Well when you whooping someone's ass so bad, I guess you don't care about where your inhaler is. And that is why his ass was six feet under now because he didn't give a fuck about me, his kids, or his health. The doctors had put him on steroids a week before his death and he was not taking the medicine. All those things factored into his death none of that had to do with me. "Well fuck him what do you want to do, do you want to have this baby?" "No I really don't," she said. "You want an abortion?" I questioned her. Cedes nodded her head. "I do." "I will go with you," I hugged her. It had been three days since Cedes had her abortion and she was not feeling good. I decided to let her stay at the house with us since she didn't want Vanessa to know what was going on. We made up a lie saying that she was going out of town for the weekend so that she could heal up. Around seven on Saturday night I heard a knock on my door I looked out the peephole and it was Vanessa. I texted Cedes to let her know that Vanessa was downstairs and to stay completely quiet, she texted back okay. By the time I made it back to my door Vanessa was banging so loud I know she had lost her mind. I opened the door with an attitude. "Damn what you trying to do get the police called on me?" I asked. "Bitch where the fuck is Cedes?" She was drunk. My kids were behind me. "Could you not use such language in front of your nieces and nephews, and come in I don't want these people in my business." I opened the door and let her in. Thankfully I had a big house so as long as Cedes stayed quiet Vanessa would not hear her. Vanessa started crying,

"I don't know what is going on it seem like Cedes is just so distant and you always be around her what is going on?" "Vanessa, I don't know what is going on Cedes is the same Cedes she always been are you sure you not mad about her independence?" Cedes had shared a little bit of information about her and Vanessa's relationship. I had to be honest it seemed as if she was controlling just like her brother. She looked at me, "my brother loved you." I smiled, "well he had a fucked-up way of showing it." Vanessa looked down at the floor. "You know he killed our Mama right in front of us. He had been beating her for years and he finally killed her." I didn't know who she was talking about, but I was listening. "How could a man say he love you but kill you. My mother was beautiful, you kind of look like her I guess that's why he loved you." I got it now she was talking about her mother and father. So, their father beat their mother that would explain a lot. I needed to hear more. "What happened Vanessa, what happened to y'all when you all where little?" I knew it had to be something deep just by the way she looked at me. It looked like she needed to get something off her chest. "Daddy beat Mama all the time. I don't know why or for how long, but he beat her. When I was thirteen and Chiquita was eighteen, Hakeem was seven, he killed her.

He stabbed her in her chest twelve times and then he shot himself in the head." Tears fell down from her face. "Daddy never liked Hakeem though he used to beat him all the time too. Hakeem was home when Daddy killed Mama and we were just grateful that he didn't kill him." That would explain a lot about Hakeem. He had been a victim also himself. That is why he really never cared for Malcolm but why name him after such a bad man. I guess he wanted to still show he loved his father, or he wanted to treat my son like his father had treated him. He had me fucked up though because he wasn't going to unleash his hatred on my son. "I know that is why Hakeem never knew how to love and Chiquita never taught him right. She was a loner who no one wanted. The only reason Lawrence is with her is because she has a lot of connections to different politicians but other than that he do not like her. No one likes her." She looked up at me, "I'm sorry my brother hit you and did you wrong." She was crying so hard that it almost made me cry. I grabbed her hand to show my appreciation. Not just for saying that but because she was letting me in on a part of Hakeem's life I didn't know about. My baby daddy had a lot of anger and pain in him. Now I understood why he was so abusive and although I understood I still was angry at him. Just because he was a victim that gave him no right to make my kids and I feel his pain. But before I knew it Vanessa had kissed me. I pulled back, she jumped up. "I'm sorry it will never happen again." She said and headed towards the door. "I really do love Cedes and I am so sorry I hit her, but I really do love her." Vanessa was the one who hit Cedes. I wonder how long the abuse was going on? I closed the door behind Vanessa and went back into the living room. I was happy that I knew the past of Hakeem and now I really understood but understanding was not the same as it being okay. I was mad because Cedes had lied to me Lawrence didn't hit her it was Vanessa. After thinking about it I guess she was too embarrassed to tell me that Vanessa had hit her. Plus, she knew she was going back so why stir things up, some things are better left unsaid. I went upstairs and got my kids ready for bed. Cedes was sleeping in Deena's room and she came out when she heard the bathroom water running. "What did she say?" She said. She was looking cute as usual her eye was healing up and she had on her purple robe. "Nothing she just needed someone to talk too." I said. "Okay she do get depressed." Cedes was content with that and she went to lay back down. I felt so sorry for her. She was so beautiful, and she didn't have anyone in this world but Vanessa, her kids, and me. I could see how she fell into the cycle of being a victim. She was getting beat by Hakeem and now Vanessa. Yup the life of being abused had its ups and downs and I am sure that Vanessa had hit her before and was going to hit her again. I knew from experience that just because you said you wanted things to change that meant nothing. Things you say never mattered until you did it, and you had to do it on your own. I had thought about leaving Hakeem and I had only left him once when he beat me but it was more because he cheated on me but that was the only time, I left him. He would beat me I would fix myself up and go lay next to him, sometimes I would even make love to him. I would get on top of him and kiss him or I would give him some head. I would feel so unloved that having sex with him would make me feel like he still loved me. He never turned me down he never told me no. No matter how mad he was he always made love to me and it made me feel like that counted for something. That he could never reject me because he was in love with me. I know it sounded stupid, but years of abuse had my head all fucked up. I loved the man who hit me. I loved the man who berated me. I loved the man who didn't love my child. I loved the man who thought he could hit my child. But that day, that was the day that I lost my mind. The day that he felt like he was going to treat my son the way he treated me. The day he felt like he was going to treat my son how he had been treated. That was the day he died was the day I lost my mind or maybe I had really found it.

Chapter Nineteen
ANIYA

"Hakeem I am getting tired of your bullshit!" I screamed. He slapped me to the floor I didn't even stay there five seconds I jumped back up. "Muthafucka you been hitting me so long that shit don't hurt!" I screamed and he punched me in my stomach. I doubled over in pain. "Bitch keep playing with me and I will fuck around and kill your ass." He grabbed my head and rammed it into the wall. I woke up out of my sleep. The reoccurring dreams of Hakeem had been replaying in my head for the last week. I did not know if it had to do with the fact that it was his birthday soon or what. Hakeem would have been turning thirty, I think I was feeling guilty. I got up and went to the box in my closet where I kept all my memories. I had Malcolm's and Deena's ultrasound. It still baffled me why he would want to name his kids after his mother and father. Why would you want your son to be named after a man that killed your mother? I understood the reasoning behind naming Deena after his mother, but it was still was confusing. I never really understood the reason why he never told me about his other three kids that he had with Cedes. Her boys were great the eldest was fifteen now and the second oldest was fourteen and the youngest was twelve. I don't know why he disowned them and disclaimed them. Cedes said it was because he didn't want any boys, he adored girls. I could see that because he did adore Deena and since he had sisters I understood that. What I couldn't understand was why did he beat on women? It was like he had his father embedded in him. I came across the piece of paper that I was looking for. It was Hakeem's obituary. It read Hakeem Ernest Harris. Born on May 7, he was a Taurus and his stubbornness was a tell-tale sign of his zodiac. Chiquita had put a picture of him when he was a little boy, a teenager, and an adult on the front cover. He was handsome. My son looked just like his daddy when he was a young boy. In the picture where he was a young boy, he wasn't smiling he was just staring into the camera with no feeling. He had a lot pain that he was hiding when he was a young boy you could tell in his eyes. That was one thing Hakeem barely smiled. He always looked serious like he had a lot on his mind, and I am sure he did. He was a victim also who became a product of his environment. I loved my baby daddy he took me from a fucked-up situation but put me into an even more fucked up situation. I know he loved me he showered me with gifts, and he took care of me and I knew that he loved me and our kids. He had gone through so much abuse and depression that he didn't know how to show his love the right way. I know he loved me because he rescued me from that fucked up situation. I started crying. I looked at his older picture on his obituary. He was so young, so handsome and ready to conquer the world. I remember listening to him at night on a good night I would lay on his chest and hear that whistling in his lung. He had the best ideas and he had the best plans. He was the reason I went to school for business because he really did inspire me. He told me I could be whatever I wanted to be he did build me up but at the same time he broke me down. I was confused on why he was beating me but now I truly understood he couldn't help it I wish I would have known to get him help. I never went to the police for when he beat and abused me, he beat me five years out of the seven years we were together he beat me. He tormented me and I never went and pressed charges I was in love. I always thought that he was going to eventually change. He told me he was going to change numerous times and he would be okay for a week or so, but he would get right back to the same things. I knew he could change because when I was pregnant with Deena, he didn't hit me. The things he did were because he wanted too. I looked at the obituary and saw how Chiquita named Deena and Malcolm as his children but not his other three boys. She knew that he had three other kids and she was that much of a bitch. She put her and Vanessa's name in the obituary and their mother and father, but she didn't put my name in the obituary. I know she was mad because I was his beneficiary and had all the rights to his money. Hell, we were together for seven years we were damn near married. Vanessa had told me a little about their childhood, but Chiquita knew more. Why did she think it was okay for her brother to beat on women? I was going to make it a goal to see what was going on with her. She had moved into the apartment that we once lived in and I was going to pay Ms. Chiquita a visit. She was the eldest and I wanted to know what happened to them. The next morning, I got a late start because I was up thinking about Hakeem. Cedes was on time and came and took the kids to school. Yes, she was still my assistant and she was great. She still came in with bruises and bumps, but I never said anything. She wanted to live like that then that was her. I know it was more to Mercedes Taylor than what she allowed people to know. I had grown fond of her and the boys. We were like a family. Some days they would come by and have dinner with us. We went out to the movies and the mall and had fun. Vanessa thought we were dating or having sex and I had to explain to her that I was strictly dickly. Bruce called me that afternoon to see if I wanted to go on a lunch date. He had been trying to get me out all the time. Honestly I was not ready to date it was too soon, but I did like Bruce and maybe one day I would give him a chance. Cedes thought I should, and I thought she was crazy. We were piled up with work and all she could talk about was how Bruce could change my life. Yes, I knew that he could, and I was taking advantage of all his connects. I was planning on expanding my business to another state and Bruce was going to help me. Cedes and I was doing the payroll since it was towards the end of the month. Payroll was stressful and I really needed to hire an accountant to do it but right now I was going to do it since I was trying to save money.

"Do you miss him?" Cedes asked and I knew she was talking about Hakeem. "Of course," I answered honestly. "I do too sometimes for real," she said looking to see my reaction, but I said nothing. "I mean he was fine girl." She laughed and I laughed too. She was right he was fine. "Girl the sex though was good as hell." I said and I meant it. He had some good sex and the head was better. "Girl the head was good," she said, and we laughed. "We were young having some fantastic flexible sex giirrrl he was bending me all different ways." She said laughing. "Oh, he got that damn flexible idea from you! Figures yo damn skinny ass. He was trying to bend me in all type of ways I was like boy no!" We giggled. "Girl I was surprised to see he had a woman as pretty as you, hell girl I know he fine but I also know he had problems." "Speaking of that why none of you heifers told me he was crazy?" I asked. "Girl please he wasn't about to beat my ass again." She joked. "Well why are you allowing Vanessa to hit you now?" I asked and she stopped laughing. "What? She don't," she shook her head. I walked over to her and knelt down in front of her. "Cedes it's me girl I endured it for five years I know a broken woman." Once I said that the water works started. I got up and grabbed a Kleenex off my desk and gave it to her. "Niya I promise she just started. I think she know about

Lawrence and she starting to treat me different." Mercedes was physically a beautiful woman but right now she looked tired and battered. "You don't have to take that abuse Cedes. Leave! Leave! Leave please!" I pleaded with her. She didn't say anything, and I knew that she wasn't. I loved Cedes like a sister, but I knew that I couldn't make her leave. It had to be her choice. I didn't have anyone to talk to when I was getting abused, but she had me. It was like we were in the same boat Vanessa had built her up and taken her in and felt as if she owned her. Vanessa had no reason to beat Cedes before because she stayed at home but, now she was getting out and was no longer under her wing. Vanessa was just like her brother I needed to know what they had been through I needed to talk to Chiquita.

Chapter Twenty

ANIYA

Today was the day and I was nervous. I didn't think that Chiquita would do anything to me, but I was nervous about the things that I would find out. Cedes was still fucking around with Lawrence against my better judgment but it gave me a chance to know Chiquita's schedule. It was Friday morning which meant she worked from home from what Lawrence had told Cedes. She was a well-known fashion designer. On Fridays she made sure all her orders were correct for Monday morning delivery. It was a sunny day, but the clouds were out heavy. It seemed as if it wanted to rain but the sun kept peeking through the clouds. I was ready to get the whole thing over with, but I had to mentally prepare my mind. I said a prayer "heavenly father please give me the information I need to move forward with my life. Although it may be difficult for me to take in give me the strength like you have done so many times. Allow me to take it in, accept it, and move on. In Jesus name Amen." I wanted to know the truth, but I was also afraid of it. I did not know what Chiquita was going to tell me, but I was preparing myself for the worst. I had endured molestation, rape, and abuse but I had survived it and it made me stronger. Hakeem had endured something, and it made him weak. Not as a person but as a man. We all go through things in life I had to learn that everyone goes through things it is how you come out of the situation that is what counts. I feel like I came out a fighter, ready to conqueror the world with no strings attached. Hakeem came out of his situation a fighter with baggage. All the things he went through he held on to it and brought it along for the ride. No matter how successful he was he was always going to think back on the life he had. I wanted to know what life had given to him that he just couldn't seem to shake off. I knew the only person who could tell me that was his sister. The woman who raised him once his mother was gone. The woman who he looked up to and looked to for advice, she had the answers to all my questions. I knew that for sure.

Chiquita was always business minded just like Hakeem. She did what she had to do to get to the top. I know for sure she loved her brother and sister to death whatever he had gone through they went through together. I put on my gray sweatpants and a black shirt. I made sure I had my short hair slicked down and put my black Adidas on my feet. I was ready just in case Chiquita felt like she wanted to fight I was going to be ready to rumble. I didn't wear any jewelry. I pulled up to my old home the home that I shared with Hakeem for so many years. It was an okay apartment building that had good tenants they definitely stayed out of people's business because as much as Hakeem and I would fight no one ever called the police. I remember Mrs. Randolph the older lady from downstairs caught me one day in the hallway after one of our many fights. I had the kids with me that Saturday we were going to a museum. Mrs. Randolph was a black woman with gray hair, and I adored her. Sometimes just to get away I would sit on her patio with her and just watch the birds. I know she heard all the yelling and fighting until this particular day. Mrs. Randolph was at her mailbox I spoke, "hey Miss lady" I said being friendly. "Don't hey miss lady me today young lady." She said in a real nasty tone. She had on a flowery yellow shirt that particular day. I didn't know what to say she had never spoke to me like that. I was going to walk pass her because I felt like she was having a bad day, but she stopped me. "Your ignorance is going to cost you and those children. Open your eyes and decide what is important him, them, or you. The Lord don't make no mistakes honey we go through things to learn and move on don't stay stuck in one place. It is okay to play the fool role once or twice, but it gets old." "Excuse me," was all I could say as I pushed past her. She had never once said anything about our fighting, and I knew that she heard it since she stayed right downstairs from us. I didn't think she was judging me, but I felt what she was saying to me was something I needed to hear but at that time I just didn't know. She was telling me that although I can keep playing the victim role it comes a time and place where we all must admit our wrong in certain circumstances. I needed to recognize that although I wasn't doing the abuse I was just as bad as Hakeem. I was allowing it to happen while doing nothing to stop especially allowing my kids to see the violence. I understood that I was in the wrong as well. That was a couple days before Hakeem died. She was right I needed to make a choice and that day the Lord made that choice for me. I made my way up to my old apartment and it still looked nice. I still had the keys, so I let myself in the hallway door. It still smelled the same also. The lady on the first floor Ms. Janet she was a widower and she grew her own flowers. She always had the place smelling so nice. I made my way up to the second floor to apartment 214. The day we moved into this apartment I was so happy. I was pregnant with Malcolm and we had been looking all over for a place that I wanted. It was perfect too. It had a eat-in kitchen, dining area, the master bedroom had a bathroom and there was another bathroom. Hakeem was about tired of me and my picky choices. "Damn baby if you don't like this place then we staying in our old place. I got shit to do I ain't got time to be riding around doing this shit." He said and it was more of a playful tone then a mad tone he was having a good day that day. "I know baby and I really do appreciate it. You take good care of me and spoil me so much baby. You know I can't do anything without my king's approval. So that other stuff just need to wait because we need a beautiful house and I need your approval." I said kissing his hand. See I could say thing like that to him one day and he would be putty in my hands, but I tried that shit when I was looking for a car and things was the opposite. He had to take me looking for a car because I didn't want anyone to bamboozle me plus he had the money. He said,

"Damn Niya I ain't go time to be out her fucking looking for cars and shit there is money to be made you couldn't do this shit yourself?" His tone was full of anger. I don't see why he was so damn mad I had just gave him my whole check from my mother's death and he couldn't take me to look for a car. But I remained calm and gentle. I said, "Baby you know I need my king's stamp of approval on what type of car I get. Hell, you know you will get in my ass if I get something that is not worth the money. You take care of me you spoil me baby, so I need to make sure you agree with the car I get." Instead of the sweet response I got like before when we was looking for an apartment he said this. "Bitch you so damn stupid you can't look for a car. Talking about you need my stamp of approval shit just say it your ass is too dumb to find a car. Did your Mama drop you on the head while those men were molesting you? Ugh you so damn stupid." See there was always was a different response and I never knew which one I was going to get. I knocked on the door and put my hand over the peephole of the door. I had a key just in case the bitch didn't want to answer the door. I heard Chiquita walking to door. I was nervous I didn't want to fight but I would if I had to. Chiquita screamed, "who is it?" I said nothing. I heard her swearing under her breath and at the same time unlocking the door. This was the moment of truth. When she saw me, she rolled her eyes. "Quita I ain't come here on no bullshit I just really want to talk. Can I please come in?" I said with my hands in the air. To my surprise she let me in without an argument. When I walked in, I saw that she had changed the place much to my amazement. It looked nice but it was dark. The living room furniture was black, and the drapes were dark. I walked to the couch and sat down. "You want something to drink?" She asked as she made her way into my kitchen. I felt odd though this had been my home for a long time, but it didn't feel homey. It never did it felt strange. My home I had built and designed to my liking felt like a home, it was our home. "No thank you," I said in fear that she would put something in my drink. She must have read my mind. "I didn't know you was coming so I couldn't have made a poisonous drink so are you thirsty or not?" I laughed same old Chiquita she knew I was paranoid hell she knew me I just didn't know her. "No, I am good for real." I said although I was really thirsty. "Fine," she said. She came back with what looked like some cold sweet tea. "How is my niece and nephew?" She asked sipping her tea. It looked like she had gained a couple of pounds she might have been eating her depression away. "They are good they need to see you."

I said and I meant every word I wanted her to have a relationship with them. "I know I just been so busy," she said and looked at a picture of Hakeem that she had on the table. "Chiquita for real I did not kill your brother," I said and that was somewhat true. "I know," she said with tears falling from her eyes. "I had to blame someone besides myself" that is when she broke down. She was crying so hard that she was farting and hiccupping. Her huge shoulders were heaving up and down and it made me cry. I went over to the couch and sat next to her. I hugged her tight. I hugged her like I loved her. I hugged her because I felt her pain not the loss, of her brother but the pain of not knowing why these things had happened to us. She calmed down I was ready to get it over with. "Quita what happened why was Hakeem like that?" She just looked at me and didn't say anything. "Vanessa told me your Daddy killed your mother." I said seeing if that would get a rise out of her and it did. "Vanessa told you a little piece of information. She didn't tell you everything and you searching for answers now?" She dried her face. "Yes," I said. She just looked at me and didn't say anything. I didn't know if I was ready to hear what she had to say but I came for answers and I wasn't leaving until I got them. I think she was trying to read me to see if I was prepared. When she didn't say anything, I felt I had to convince her I was ready. "Come on Quita I went through five years of abuse from your brother and I have his kids. Speaking of kids why didn't anyone tell me about his other three kids?" I wanted her to feel guilty. "You owe me this I love you; I love your brother. I want to know what pain and hurt he had been feeling all them years for him to turn out the way that he did, please tell me." I said. She got up and went to the kitchen. She came back with a big bottle of Brandy. "Okay but I am definitely going to need a drink to relive this bullshit." She took a sip. I felt the need to feel at peace and I took a shot of Brandy too. The taste burned my throat. I wanted her to feel at ease, so I drank some shots with her. After about ten shots I knew she was ready. I braced myself and got myself together so that I could take in all the information.

Chapter Twenty-One
CHIQUITA

Lord knows that I did not want to relive this shit, but I felt like I did owe Niya since my brother did love her. The way he showed his love wasn't right but shit that is how we was brought up. I loved my brother he was the apple of my eye and everything he did I condoned. Maybe if I had not condoned his behavior then he would still be alive. My Mama was a very pretty woman. She had big hips and legs just like me and Niya. She was light skinned like Niya but Vanessa and I were brown like Daddy. Hakeem had inherited those gray eyes that Daddy had though. Those eyes still haunted me to this day that is why sometimes I loved my brother but sometimes I hated him because I saw my father in him. "He molested me," I blurted out to Niya she was sitting there looking at me like I was crazy. "I guess you can relate to that too from what Hakeem told me about your Mother's boyfriend molesting you. I think I endured worse because he was my father." She turned and looked at me and I had tears in my eyes. "I don't hate you Niya but I do think there was more to my brother's death. I know he was wrong I know that, but I loved my brother and he loved me. I just can't accept the fact that he is gone." I know what they say when you try to act like you and your problems are bigger than others, but I did feel like I had gone through more. Hell, he was my father and he raped me but not only that it was more to the story.

"Don't be mad at your mother for you getting molested Niya. Sometimes things that happen to us are no one's fault, and we must place the blame on the one who is doing the wrong and solely on them. I know because I hated my mother for allowing my father to molest me. He never touched Vanessa, but he molested me. For years I hated her I wouldn't even talk to my mother and now that she is gone I have so much to say. Not only did he molest me for years, but he got me pregnant too." I had tears falling from my face, but this was a long time coming. I needed to get it off my chest. I didn't have any one to talk to. I had no friends and I kept to myself. To be honest Niya was my friend and I missed her company. "Yeah at first I could have kids but after the third abortion I guess my young body couldn't take it and I never got pregnant again. I wanted to keep my babies Niya I did. The first time I got pregnant I was thirteen that is when Mama realized her worst nightmare that Daddy was for sure raping me. I think she always felt like he was doing something to me, but she never said anything until that day." I was sitting in the kitchen eating some bacon and I got the urge to vomit. I ran to the bathroom just in time and made it to the toilet. Mama came in after me. "Chiquita girl what is wrong with you?" She asked. "I don't know Mama," I said. She took me to the doctor's and her worst nightmare was confirmed I was six weeks pregnant. That was the first time I got pregnant. Then I got pregnant again at the age of fourteen. Daddy told Mama that I needed to get on birth control and Mama said no you need to quit fucking her. That was all she said he laughed at her and walked out of the room. We did the same thing before went and got an abortion but we had to go a little further out of the county so no one would ask questions on why a fourteen-year old was pregnant yet again and getting an abortion. The last time I got pregnant was a couple of months before I ran away, I was sixteen. The doctor that Mama took me too knew I had two other abortions he said Ma'am with all do, respect I do not know what is going on and why this girl keeps getting abortions, but you need to get this under control. Mama showed him the money. He told her that because I had so many abortions, I might never be able to get pregnant. I cried I told Mama that I was older, and I wanted to keep my baby she slapped me so hard that my head flew against the wall. "Shut up girl!" She yelled you not keeping nothing. She shoved the money into the doctor's hand. "You take this money and get rid of this got damn problem. You know I can find someone else to do it cheaper." He looked at me he was a young white guy. "Ma'am I know you talking about those back alley, guys and I suggest you not do that." She yelled "I don't want too! But if you leave me no choice I will!" He grabbed the money and gave me my third abortion. I was hurt so bad that I didn't know what to do. He knew if I went to those back alley, people I would have died so he did it for me. Mama was content she didn't care how bad killing my babies felt to me. "So was your Daddy hitting your Mother why was she letting him molest you?" Niya broke me out of my trance I had forgot that she was here. "Nope he wasn't hitting her at that time. He didn't start hitting Mama until after I left home at sixteen. I had been pregnant by him three times by this time and each time he gave us the abortion money. I was tired of everything. Here I was a sixteen-year old girl who couldn't date because I was getting fucked by my father." I looked at Niya and it look like my words stung her heart yes it stung mine too. "Damn," she whispered. "One day I packed my clothes in my school bag and ran away. I met a nice woman at a center for women who were in a domestic situation. Although I wasn't eighteen, I lied to her, but I think she knew I was lying since I was still in High School. She risked everything to save my life. She helped me get my own apartment. She helped me get my life on track and succeed in everything. She helped me with Hakeem when he moved with me, he adored A'Deena I was glad that he named y'all kids after Malcolm and A'Deena they were our real parents our life savers." "Wait what? A'Deena and Malcolm aren't y'all parents name?" Niya had cut me off but I knew she was in shock. "No, I thought Hakeem told you that our parents were Olivia that was my mother's name and our father's name was Edward. Hakeem hated our parents because of the way he lived. He was seven when he finally got out of that house. But it was too late for him just like it was too late for me. Although I had

Deena and Malcolm it was hard for me to cope with everyday life. I was so hurt when they died. They died when Hakeem was fourteen and he took it hard. They had been in our life for a short amount of time, but they had such an impact on us. That's where our business sense came from." "Wow," was all that Aniya could say. I know that all this information was surprising, but she was the one who wanted to hear it. "All the other things we got from our real mother and father. My mother was a mean woman to me. She didn't like me because my father was molesting me. She never said anything to him that I knew of. If she did say anything to him it made no difference because he was still molesting me. Do you know when I ran away, they didn't even bother to look for me? Vanessa told me that my mother knew exactly where I was at and she was glad that I was away." I looked at Aniya. "He loved you," I said I just had to let her know the truth the liquor was making me vulnerable. She took another shot, "I know." "I was a bit jealous of that. You were his woman and you were taking my little brother from me. I didn't really talk to Vanessa like that we were close but not as close as Hakeem and I. There was many times after he would beat you that he would come over and be crying. He would say, Quita I don't know what the fuck is wrong with me I love this woman so much and here I am giving her so much pain." "Sometimes I would yell at him but other times I would encourage him saying shit like well she need to learn to listen to you. Or I would say shit obviously you not hitting her hard enough because she still acting up. So yes, I did play a part in him beating you so for that I do apologize." "I mean damn girl look at this he left you a damn insurance policy he put your name on his businesses and his bank account and y'all wasn't even married. Yes, I am jealous I can admit that. That is why I had to take this apartment to have a little of my brother with me." She didn't say anything, and I wondered what she was thinking. "I am glad I got Lawrence he makes me not think about Hakeem so much and he made me kind of get through his death. I know he not perfect and I honestly think that he is cheating on me but look," I waved my hand in her face. "He proposed but who the hell is going to walk me down the aisle?" I started crying and just so full of myself I was really happy that he had asked for my hand in marriage and this was everyth ing I wanted. He wasn't perfect but he was for me. "Well maybe Vanessa could walk you down the aisle, hell she look like a man." Aniya joked. I started howling with laughter. "Girl I missed you," I hugged her. "I really did, and I miss the kids and I want to see them. I am sorry I treated you so wrong and didn't allow you guys to see Hakeem at the funeral." "Oh, don't trip I followed you so that I could find out where everything was, and we saw him before you guys came in." Niya responded back and I was a bit shocked. I thought she really didn't care about my brother, but I guess I was wrong. "Nobody was going to stop me from seeing my man" when she said that I knew her ass was as crazy about him as he was about her. "So how are my niece and nephew?" "They are fine getting big. That Deena keeps asking for her Father. Malcolm he is okay he understands things a little better." "Well Malcolm did see a lot of y'all fighting and although he is still young that shit still affects him. Hakeem was around four when our Daddy started beating on our Mother. And look at how bad it affected him. That cuts kids deep. You should put him in therapy. I wish I would have gotten help for Hakeem when he was that age but when he came to live with me him and Vanessa it didn't seem like he was going to be such an angry person. He would get into fist fights at school, so I guess that was a sign, but I was too young to know better. Deena and Malcolm never noticed anything because he was such an angel around them." We sat in silence for a moment. "I had it hard yes Lord I did but Hakeem was a child also and he had it tough. Our father started molesting me at the age of nine. He started beating Hakeem when he was four right after I left. He would beat him and my Mother. He would mostly beat my mother for trying to defend Hakeem. She took those beatings and allowed the beatings and she never left.

Chapter Twenty-Two
CHIQUITA

"When Hakeem got to me; he was under the normal weight he was eating so fast and stuff that he was throwing up after meals. I had to make him calm down because it wasn't healthy for him. I do not know how I had not recognized his weight lost before. I guess because I was so into my own problems; I did not have time for his but once I saw it right in my face, I knew that my little brother had suffered." I stuffed a piece of chicken in my mouth I had gotten hungry. Niya was patiently waiting for me to finish the story. "The day that my father had killed my mother was the day that she had had enough. Hakeem told me that he had been standing in the corner for two hours when my mother finally told my daddy that that was enough. Of course, daddy didn't want to hear that. Mama went to get Hakeem out of the corner and daddy struck her in the back of the head. She didn't fall or nothing. Hakeem stayed in the corner, but Mama was ready to go to war." "She ran to the kitchen and grabbed a knife. Daddy was mad and called her a bitch and told her to put the knife down or he was going to kill Hakeem. He had grabbed Hakeem out of the corner and had him by the neck. Mama was scared and did not want Hakeem to die so she dropped the knife on the counter. Daddy let Hakeem go. Once he let Hakeem go, he grabbed the knife. Mama told Hakeem to run and hide. Vanessa wasn't at the house yet. Hakeem ran and hid." Niya was staring at me intently with her eyes. I was reliving what my brother had lived through. "Hakeem thought that Daddy was just beating Mama. Hakeem stayed hidden outside on the fire escape he had closed the window so Daddy wouldn't think to look there. Daddy was searching for Hakeem when Vanessa came home from a friend's house. She found Mama on the kitchen floor bloody and lifeless. She screamed and Daddy came back to the kitchen. Vanessa was in tears and was asking our Daddy why. For some reason Vanessa was always Daddy's pick I think because she looked a lot like him. He had come off his high at that point and seen what he had done. Vanessa said he went into the room closed the door and killed himself with his gun. When the police came, they found Hakeem still outside shivering from the cold." I could tell Niya was in deep thought, but I continued talking. "Hakeem told me about all the horrific things our Father had been doing to him. How my mother would make a big meal, but Hakeem couldn't eat the food he had to sit at the table and watch everyone else eat. One day he tried sneaking food in the middle of the night and our Father made him eat dog food the next day. He would whoop him with extension cords and big thick black belts. Oh, the life he had lived at a young age was no life for a child." I was in tears and so was Aniya. "Hakeem told me all about the way our father would pour water over him and beat him until he damn near passed out. I don't know why our Father hated his son, but he did. He hated Hakeem for no reason or there was a reason, but we just never knew why. I know our Father was in foster care, so you never know what kind of treatment he himself had suffered. But to treat a child that way your child that was just cruel and nasty. Girl Hakeem would cry from night terrors trembling saying please! Please! Please don't kill me! He was in pain he was in fear and I tried to love that fear out of him. I would hold him through the night. I had to stay at school with him sometimes to make sure he was focused on work and not on his past beatings. But you just don't get over things like that. It took a while he was about ten years old when that stopped but then he had started wetting the bed until he was about twelve. I know it was because of the abuse so I never got mad I just told him we would get through it together. And that's how I always felt that no matter what Hakeem and I could get through anything together. I loved that pain out of him, but when he met Cedes it was like that behavior was trained into him. I knew it was wrong but inside of me I was not right also. I knew if I told Hakeem that he was doing wrong that he would have stopped. Something wanted me to only agree to everything he was doing. I never wanted to be negative towards him so I found a reason why he should do it. I know now that I was wrong but at the time, I wanted other people to feel my pain when I should have been trying to protect others from the pain we felt. For years I was jealous of you and Cedes you bitches took my baby brother from me the only man who loved me. Now that I have Lawrence who I can tell all my secrets too. Now that I have him who I can actually be open and in love with I know that I was being selfish." I looked Niya in her eyes "please forgive me." "I forgive but I will never forget." She told me. "I appreciate you being so honest with me so that I could move on with my life, but things could have been so different our lives could have been so much different. You need to get help you and Vanessa. Vanessa may not have gotten beaten on, but she is feeling some type of loss too you need to talk to her because she is beating on Cedes." I was shocked, "Oh no say it isn't so!" "It is so, you need to reach out to your sister and see what kind of help she needs. I don't know what her problem is, but she is hurting also." She gave me a hug and got ready to leave but I stopped her. "Niya now that I was so honest with you can you please be honest with me" I was crying I just didn't believe that she had nothing to do with my brother's death. "What happened that day?" "He had an asthma attack." She looked me in my eyes. I didn't want to believe that to be the truth. "Okay can I see my niece and nephew I really miss them." "Only if you promise to get to know your other three nephews" she got smart. "Yup you right and I will talk to Cedes about that." I agreed. "Okay and I will follow up with her about it too and if she says you went through with it then I will absolutely let you continue to be in their lives." She walked out the door. I finished what was left in my glass of

Brandy. I had spilled my heart to Aniya, yet something inside of me felt like she was lying about how my brother had died. I had to get something out of her or she would pay with her ass.

Chapter Twenty-Three

ANIYA

Malcolm was playing with his red truck in the living room and Deena was sitting by him playing with her Baby Alive doll. I was in the kitchen washing up the last dishes and Hakeem was sitting in the living room watching television. It was tension in the air, and I knew that something was going to happen. I was on my last dish and I do not know what happened, but I heard Deena cry and Hakeem scream "what the fuck!" I ran into the living room and he had Malcolm by his shirt collar. There was red juice all over Deena and the carpet, but I did not care about that he had my baby in an uncomfortable position and I did not like it. "Hakeem let him go!" I yelled. I could feel my blood boiling with anger.

He turned and looked at me while still holding Malcolm, "bitch shut the fuck up!" I could see the fire in his eyes. He was ready to beat my ass I did not care he had my son. "Let him the fuck go muthafucka or I am going to fuck you up!" I was just as angry as him, if not angrier. I did not care if I lost my life. He could beat me, belittle me, but I was going to die before I allow him to do anything to my son. He looked at like I had lost my mind. The truth was I had lost my mind I knew what Hakeem could do to me, but I also knew my own strength. "Oh, bitch you done lost your mind!" He raised up his free hand and slapped my five-year old son to the floor. Malcolm fell to the floor crying. I was light as a feather as I charged at Hakeem. I punched him twice in his mouth and drew blood. I had never hit Hakeem as many times as he had hit me and this time, I initiated the fight. He touched his lip and saw the blood. "Bitch!" He punched me in my face, and I stumbled but I didn't fall. I jumped into my kickboxing stance and was ready to rumble. He looked shocked. "Oh, so you want to fight?" All these years I had never fought back. All these years I had endured his pain, black eyes, busted lips, he stomped me out, broke my jaw, slapped me, choked me but I was not about to let him hurt my son. That was one thing I was not about to do. I did not say anything. He looked kind of scared hell I was scared. After five years of physical and mental abuse I had had enough. All I could hear was my Malcolm's cry and I was mentally prepared to battle this muthafucka to the finish. "Malcolm take your sister and go in the bathroom and lock the door. Do not open the door unless I tell you to you understand?" I said to my son as I stared at his father. Malcolm was still whimpering as he grabbed his sister and did what I told him to do. "Oh, bitch until he hear your voice. Now what if you don't make it?" When he said that I knew we was going to fight until one of us died but I was prepared I had mentally prepared myself for this brawl for months ever since I had started kickboxing. I knew it would one day come to this and I was not going to sit around and let him beat on my son. I heard the bathroom door close and lock. I knew my kids were safe. I quickly kicked Hakeem in his mouth. He looked shock once again, but he charged at me this time getting on top of me. I wasn't prepared for that, but I wrestled with him like I was a man. Hell, I had taken beating after beating like I was a man now the competition was on and we were coming for blood. He was on top of me choking me and I was damn near unconscious, but I forced my body to get life I forced myself to not be a victim any more I put my arms around his body and flipped him over and now I was on top, but I didn't stay there I jumped on my feet. Hakeem was on the ground and in fucking shock. He got to his feet and he was scared I could see it in his eyes. He didn't know what to do. He stood in front of me unprepared for what I had for him. He was like a deer caught in the headlights; he was like me the many times I got my ass beat out of nowhere. "Do not charge at me again muthafucka. Fight me like a man! You have been beating my ass all these years like I was a man so fight me like one pussy. Let's go!" I screamed. You could see the surprise on his face but then he laughed an evil horrifying laugh. "Alright bitch you tough let's go." He said. I could tell he was sad and hurt because I had never fought him back. I could see the hurt in his eyes, but I could also see the thirst for blood in his eyes too. I was ready for any outcome and if I lost my life defending my children then call me a Shero because I was not going to let him knock them around without a fight. There are too many helpless children in the world. I was a helpless child I would be damned if I continued the cycle. I would be damned if I allowed him to beat my child. Oh no this mother would not lay down like a wimp, a coward, a punk and allow her baby's father to abuse their child. This man had abused me. He had not given me a ring just words and lies. He did take care of us but at what expense hell and some of that was my money I helped build the empire. He didn't treat our kids equally and although he adored Deena he didn't take her anywhere. I went out, I bought everything for them. Yes, he gave me the money but hell I had contributed to that pot of gold. This sorry excuse for a man thought it was okay to rescue me and then turn around and harm me. He may have loved me he may have loved his kids, but he did not show it. I had fucked up I had picked a sorry excuse for a father for my children he was the real definition of a baby's daddy and not a father. This time he didn't wait for me to hit him he threw a punch and missed, and I grabbed his arm and pushed him onto the ground. He seemed stunned as he got up and stared at me for a long time. He looked me in my eyes and his look was confusion and for a moment I was ready to call the whole thing off but then I thought back to when he slapped Malcolm and I knew that this abuse was going to get worse. "What you waiting for?" I asked. He walked up on me and pushed me, but I didn't budge. I kneed, him in the stomach quickly and did a quick left jab to his face. He looked mad. "Nigga I am not playing with your ass! You usually be ready to fight. Fight me." I made sure to control my voice so that no one could hear me. "Why you wanna fight me Niya?" He asked me. Fuck that he had whooped my ass too many times. I punched him twice in his face. "The same reason you been whooping my ass because I feel like it. Don't be scared now pussy." I punched him again. He stepped back at that moment when he realized wasn't no talking, we were going to fight. We were both in a fight stance and I knew at that moment it had gotten real. Hakeem threw three punches at my face and two connected. His hits were hard and fast, so I was winded, but I stood my ground. We were swinging on each other so fast and hard you would have thought we were enemies. Not that we had lived together for seven years and had two beautiful children. No, we were throwing hits so hard and fast at each other you would have thought we owed each other not that we had just made love last night and had dinner less than ten minutes ago. Nope we were on a mission and between the both of us we were like lions; who would be crowned king? I tripped over the couch a bit and Hakeem caught me on the side of my face and I knew I had a bruise on my jaw. I grabbed his shirt when I fell so that he could not choke me again because I knew if he did then I might not have enough strength to get up. We rolled all over the couch tussling and struggling we were both trying to win. Just then Hakeem started wheezing. "Niya stop." He said out of breath and I let him go. He was trying to get air. "I need my asthma pump." Hakeem was out of breath. I saw the pain in his eyes, and I started looking for the damn pump. I got to the back of the house where I had hid his asthma pump in Malcolm's drawer. I went to open the drawer but then my mind flooded with all those memories. The hurt, the pain, and then I looked at the pictures of my kids. I had to go through with it. It was working and I had to go through with it. I closed the door back and ran to the bathroom door. "Open the door Malcolm." I heard him turn the knob and I opened the door and grabbed my son and daughter and locked the door behind us. I got in the bathtub. I could hear Hakeem get up and come looking for me or maybe he was looking for his asthma pump. He didn't have his nebulizer anymore because he had gotten mad a couple of months ago and threw it at me and it no longer worked. I prayed at that moment that God would not let him find his asthma pump. I could hear him walking through the house throwing things, but he wasn't talking so I knew he was having trouble breathing. All we could hear was bumps and thumps and the kids and I stood still. This was not the first time we had locked ourselves in the bathroom while Hakeem had went on a rampage, so they were used to this. They had no idea that Hakeem was not on rampage to destroy the house, but he was on a rampage looking for his lifeline. After about five minutes I heard a loud crash and I knew it was Hakeem's lifeless body. But I didn't move.

Chapter Twenty-Four
ANIYA

I jumped up out of my sleep sweating. I had not thought about that day and this was the first time that the day events had played through my mind. I went into my master bathroom to use the bathroom. I looked in the mirror and my face was red. I put some cold water on my face. I went into Deena's and Malcolm's room to check on them. They were doing okay. I went back to my room and laid down. I closed my eyes and the events came back. I stayed in the bathroom for a good thirty minutes before deciding to go out and check on Hakeem. I walked through the hall and into the bedroom where I heard the crash. There he was on the floor. I screamed "No! Hakeem get up!" The tears started flowing. I grabbed my cell phone on the bed and called 911 I was hysterical. The ambulance came in about ten minutes. They tried to resuscitate him, but he wasn't responding. I sat on the side and held my kids the entire time praying that he did not wake up. Yes, on the outside I looked like a mourning baby mama but on the inside, I was jumping for joy. They pronounced him dead at 7:55 pm and I was relieved. Of course, they took me in for questioning because they saw how our house looked and they saw my face and the scar on Hakeem's face where I had kicked him. I explained to them how he and I were fighting. I got loose from him and ran into the bathroom with my kids. I thought he was having a tantrum like he had done so many times before. I thought he had left when I didn't hear anything anymore and I left out the bathroom to find him on the bedroom floor dead. The most important question they kept asking "was he having an asthma attack before you went in the bathroom?" My answer every time was no. I thought I was going to go to jail but thankfully when they interviewed the neighbors, they told them about all the abuse I had gone through. No, I didn't have anything documented but I had witnesses of the abuse. The detective contacted Chiquita who from the start questioned everything and felt like they should arrest me. She didn't care about all the pain her brother had caused me all she cared about was the pain I caused her. The detectives had to explain to her that they would be doing an autopsy, but it looked like my story checked out. They even asked her did she know about the abuse and she sat in my face and denied ever knowing. I woke up feeling a bit drained. I knew why I was thinking about Hakeem and what had happened. Today was his thirtieth birthday. I got my kids dressed and Cedes said that she would meet me at the cemetery. All three of us dressed in all black to mourn the loss of their father. Although I had that dream, I still did not feel guilty and after learning all the things that Chiquita had told me about Hakeem's childhood, I knew that I had put him out of his misery, and he was at peace. He was a man living in pain that was not going to go away. The truth was if I had not taken him out then he would have took me out. Chiquita showed up at the cemetery also. I hugged her to everyone's surprise, and she had Lawrence with her. She looked good she had some long wavy weave in her hair, and she had worn black also. You could tell that Cedes was uncomfortable being around Lawrence and Chiquita since she was still sleeping with Lawrence but today was not about her it was about Hakeem. Chiquita was crying but she wanted to speak "I miss you so much baby brother"

Lawrence was holding her hand. "I know that I have failed you, but I do not want to fail your kids all five of them." She turned at Cedes. "I am sorry, and I acknowledge your kids also." You could tell that shocked Cedes but she hugged Chiquita and accepted her apology. No one else said anything we were all content with what Chiquita said. The kids were being strong I don't really think Deena knew what was going on and where we were at. Vanessa had not come with us she said she would do it on her own, she was so distant. Her and Cedes were not doing good but I know once Chiquita talked to her about hitting on Cedes she had stopped. At first Cedes was upset because I had told Chiquita and she did not talk to me for a week, but she came around. We released the balloons and parted ways. I had some business to take care so I allowed the kids to go with Chiquita I know she could use their company. Not only that but I know they missed their Auntie. I pulled up at the office on 3rd street and looked it over. It looked like a dump to say the least. I got out and walked to the building I hope Sarah had given me the right information I should have called. The glass door was open when I reached for it, so I pulled it open. The lobby was poorly lit and there was no receptionist. "Hello!" I yelled out and it echoed. "Yes, can I help you?" The all too familiar voice called back. I didn't say anything I just walked to my right where I heard the voice. There was an open wooden door there and I stepped in. There he was sitting at the desk I smiled. "Niya!" He said. He got up from the circle desk. His 6'3 frame looked big as it always had and he looked good in his suit. We embraced and I sat in the chair. "Sarah gave me your address." I said smiling from ear to ear. "Good where did you run into her at?" He asked while going back around the desk and sitting in his chair. "The mall," I said. "It must have been meant." "Yes, that is for sure. You look great," He said giving me the once over. I was glad he recognized my look. "I feel great too." I said and he knew what I meant. "Anyways I know you didn't want any payment but here." I said handing him an envelope. "What's this?" He asked. "Ten thousand dollars." "Come on now I can't take this" he tried to hand it back to me. "No take it that is the least I could do after all you have done for me." He looked at me, "so it worked?" was all he asked. "Yeah" I stated quickly, "look I came into a lot of money and I know you are trying to get your business off the ground all I want to do is help." I got up to leave. "Niya" he said, and I turned around "thank you." "No thank you." I meant every word of it. I got back in my car and headed home I needed a nice hot bath after the day I had. I would never admit to anyone that I had planned the death of Hakeem. No, I would never admit it out loud. Only one person knew what I had done and that was Chance. I got in my hot bubble bath and thought back to when I had met Chance. He was a guy in my business class. We took a couple classes together since we had the same major. I had been seeing him all the years I had been in school. He had seen me too. The battered me, the smart me, the real me. He was my friend and I loved him for helping me. He was the only person who understood what I was going through and he was the only person that helped me figure out what I should do. So, ten thousand dollars of money to help him was nothing because the help he gave me was priceless.

Chapter Twenty-Five
ANIYA

Chance was a brown skinned God. He was beautiful from head to toe. He had been in a couple of my classes since I had started school, but we had never spoken. I was too afraid to talk to men because I didn't know what Hakeem would do to me if he found out. We had a mutual classmate Sarah Devule. Sarah was a white girl with short brown hair. She wasn't that pretty, but it was something about her that made you take a second glance it was something about her that made her a beauty. Sarah and I had teamed up to work on a class project. I loved working with Sarah she kept me laughing. She was the only person I had talked to as a friend besides

Mya and Chiquita. Sarah was going to school to study law, but her minor was business and that is how we met. Chance and Ralph were in another group and they sat by us in the library. Sarah seemed to have a thing for Chance, but she would say "if my parents knew I would date a black man my life would be over." Sarah was funny everyone wanted to be her friend but for some reason she clung to me. She would say, "I like you because you listen to all that I have to say." She liked to talk and talk and talk about nothing but since I was going through so much and needed the distraction I would listen. She knew that Hakeem was abusing me too, but I didn't tell her she just knew. I walked in the women's bathroom at school one day and Sarah was in there. I smiled and she smiled back. Hakeem had busted my lip and it hurt really badly and I know people could see it. The swelling had gone down but there was a cut still on my lip. She looked at me and she said, "I know how you can cover that up." I just looked at her in embarrassment, but I didn't say anything I just waited while she looked in her purse. She pulled out black lipstick. "This right here will cover it up." She started applying the lipstick to my lips. "Don't worry I know all about these little accidents my mother had enough of these accidents." I still didn't say anything. "There," she stated, and I looked in the mirror and you could not see my busted lip anymore I started crying. She hugged me and it made me cry harder. I was so worried because here I was coming in with another busted lip. I was always coming to school beat up and maybe that is why Sarah befriended me because she wanted to help me. We were in the library and once again Hakeem had beaten my ass. My eye was black, and I thought the makeup I had, had concealed it well but Chance kept staring at me. Sarah was talking and talking but I could feel Chance's eyes staring, burning a hole through my makeup. We were about to head out when Chance stopped me. "Aye hold up!" He yelled to me. I stopped because Sarah was with me, so I felt better. Just in case Hakeem was watching somewhere. I know he watched me sometimes because he would say things that only a person who had seen me that day would say. Chance was bald with a shiny head. His buff built body was beautiful even through his shirt I could see his muscles. "Here," he said handing me a piece of paper. I looked at the paper and I think that he knew I was getting the wrong idea. "Just call it's nothing like that I want to help," and he walked away. I didn't know what to think had Sarah been telling people about me getting beat. No, it wasn't her fault even if she had been telling people hell, they could see the abuse from the scars she had been helping me hide. It took me two weeks to call Chance and I called him from a payphone. He told me to meet him at his downtown loft and we could get started. Get started on what I had no clue. I used Sarah as an alibi to get out of the house that Saturday. Although the kids were gone over Chiquita's house Hakeem expected me to stay and look at his ass all day. It wasn't like we were going on a date. I met up with Chance at his loft he had given me the address at school. He never stopped and talked long he just had a note with this address. His loft was very spacious and that was good for what we were about to do. I had on some yoga pants with a tee shirt something comfortable. I knew I needed to be comfortable, but I didn't know why. We were sitting at his kitchen table and he had some water and fruits for us to eat and drink. He hadn't said anything he just opened the door and let me in. "I am so glad you came," he smiled at me. I still said nothing. "Look I don't know you Niya but I have been seeing you for years. Everyone has been seeing you for years. They have been talking, talking about your bruises." I knew people were talking I put my head down and shame and tears fell from my eyes. "Hey now don't cry." He said. He went out of the room and came back a few minutes later. "This is my sister Carla." He showed me a picture of a beautiful girl she looked Puerto Rican though. "How is this your sister?" I asked. "We were both adopted by the same family. I have known and loved Carla since I was a child. She was the only family I had besides Mama and Daddy. She was my best friend and I no longer have her." The tears fell from his eyes. "My sister Carla had been in an abusive relationship for the past three years and that bastard killed her. None of us knew about it she just distanced herself from us. One day we got that call to come and identify her body. That was three weeks ago. And I see you Niya so young so beautiful and I know I can't let his continue. Tell me your story." I had dried my eyes and I was ready to open up. He didn't seem like he wanted to use my past against me he seemed genuine like he wanted to help. I told him everything even about James. "What do you want Niya?" His question took me by surprise. No one had asked me what I wanted to do about the situation with Hakeem ever. I didn't have an answer. "Look I know you may not be able to answer that right-away so right now I just want to show you ways to protect yourself. Okay?" That was how my kickboxing lessons started. Every Saturday I would lie and tell Hakeem that I was going to yoga classes with Sarah and Sarah told me she would agree to keep the lie going. She made sure she texted me every Friday night and Saturday morning just in case Hakeem ever looked in my phone. Hell, she would meet up with me before I went to see Chance just so that we could talk pictures. She would send me the photos just in case Hakeem ever got suspicious. She was a great friend. After about three months of taking lessons I was good at it. I mean really good as big as I was, I could kick my legs high and I could move fast. It was one Thursday that changed everything in me. I was learning to defend myself but what happened made me want to kill Hakeem. I was in the bathtub getting some relaxation time to myself. Deena had fallen asleep, but Malcolm was still awake watching television. Hakeem was in the room ironing his clothes for work. He thought I was going to do it, but I told him I needed to get in the tub and after that I was going to bed. He looked pissed but he didn't hit me. It seem like he hadn't thought of a cruel enough way to get at me. I heard Malcolm scream and it made me jump up I guess I had fallen asleep in the tub. I got out of the tub and was wrapping my towel around my body. I heard Hakeem go in the room with Malcolm, so I took my time, but I was listening "What's wrong boy?" He questioned. "I saw a spider Dad." Malcolm said. I laughed awwww my baby scared of a little spider. "Boy your little punk ass in her screaming like a little bitch over a spider." Those were some harsh words to say to a five-year old. "But Dad it is big." He said. "Sissy I am not your Daddy not saying sissy shit like that. Take your fag ass to bed before I beat your ass for screaming like that!" He yelled and I could hear him storm out the room and I could also hear my baby crying. I quickly got dressed and went to Malcolm. I cuddled my son and let him know his mother was here for him. "Mama it really was a big spider." He cried and I wanted to cry too but I didn't I had cried enough. "I know baby fuck him." I growled and I meant it. I had been with Hakeem for seven years and Malcolm was five. He had never hit Malcolm or anything he just didn't show him any attention. I knew that his hatred for Malcolm was growing just like his hatred for me had grown. It had taken time for him to start beating me. I knew it was just a matter of time before he started hitting my son and that was going to be the day that I challenged him. That was going to be the day that I was going to war. I was going to prove to him the difference between being a mother and being a baby mama was all about. Hakeem had told me many times that all I was, was a baby mama because I lived off of him. I took his money. I couldn't even support my kids without him was what he said. Maybe he was right about that, but I was a mother a damn good one at that. I spent time with my children, I read to them, I took them to places, I cooked, and all of their needs came before mines. The only need that I had that I needed to get rid of was his sorry ass and after that I would be a better mother than before. I told Chance my plan and he thought it was a great idea. I told him I felt that Hakeem was going to start hitting Malcolm and Chance thought that he was going to too. I told him about Hakeem having asthma and how he didn't really take care of himself. I watched the movie Enough with Jennifer Lopez and it helped me develop a plan. I devised a plan it wasn't premeditated I was going to be prepared it was not going to be deliberate it was going to be precise. If he tried to harm us in any way, I would kill him with precision. The day that Hakeem put his hands on, Malcolm was the day that I was going to fight his ass. He didn't know about my kickboxing lessons because I still would not fight him back. No, I was going to make him wait for this ass whooping. I knew that Chance would have beaten Hakeem's ass for me, but I needed to do it on my own. All of that would have done is caused tension in the household. Yes, I could leave but then what he would harass me and follow me. I needed to do this on my own. Chance was a blessing, but I knew that he had ulterior motives behind helping me kill Hakeem. I knew for a fact that Hakeem was cheating on me with Chance's girlfriend. He had been for years and I know that Chance knew that. I saw the texts in Hakeem's phone with them going back and forth. Yes, Chance had used me, but he had helped me also. I had grown fond of Chance by the time I had found out all the information. I never said anything to Chance because all in all shit he was my way out. The reason I paid him was for hush money because I wanted to make sure this all stayed a secret. People say that they don't need money, but the truth is they do. I didn't know why Chance was still with his girlfriend but that was his problem the heart makes the mind do things that we cannot comprehend. I knew that if I tussled with Hakeem that he would have an asthma attack and wouldn't be able to breathe. That was my plan to blame the asthma and him beating on me that was going to be the reason he died. I just wanted to tussle with him enough to keep me alive and to make him have an asthma attack that was the plan and it worked. I didn't have any documentation of him hitting me so I knew that causing an asthma attack would keep me out of jail. It worked too and I was happy. No more living in fear, no more feeling ashamed. I was going to live my life with my kids. I had endured so much pain over the years I was happy it was over. I didn't know what my future held but I knew that it was going to be better than what my past had given me. Yes, Chiquita had helped me to realize that Hakeem had been through some pain, but it also helped me realize I had done the right thing. He would have beaten me until my death, and I did not need that my kids needed their mother. I got my kids and snuggled with them in my bed that night. It felt so good! I was in love all over again and this time it was real. My kids were my everything I had taken so much that I needed to feel safe again. My baby daddy had given me these gifts of life and for that I will be forever grateful, but he had also taken so much from me and I had taken it back. With the help of God, my children, and love I was going to restore my life. Bruce had asked me out again an I felt like I was ready to date him. He had showed me that he was a genuine person. I didn't see any red flags that would make me think that he would harm me or my kids. I would give him a try plus what is the worst that could happen. I already had to kill my baby daddy. I don't think I would have to kill my boyfriend, or would I? To Be Continued…

ABOUT THE AUTHOR

New York Times & International Best Selling Author Billie Dureyea Shell was born in Compton California and now lives in Ladera Heights with his wife and kids who he loves to spend time with.

He is the Owner of several properties in the Los Angeles area and gives back to his community by providing low income housing to those who need it.

He stated "It doesn't matter where you at or where you from it's what you do with your time. There's nothing you can't do if you put your mind to it".

COMING SOON
SEPTEMBER 2020